Amy reached down and turned the frame over. The picture within it was hard to see in the depths of the drawer. Amy lifted it out into the sunlight and felt her whole body tingle in shock.

"Oh, my God."

Two guys stared out of the frame at her, one dark, one blond. The blond one's blue eyes twinkled with mischief at the camera. One elbow leaned casually on the shoulder of the dark-haired guy at his side.

Amy closed her eyes. In the silence of her mind, she conjured up an image, the face she'd been drawing for months now. The face she'd drawn just the night before, trapped inside a coffin. When she opened her eyes, the dark eyes of the guy in the photo looked back.

Nick Granger was the guy she'd met so briefly, yet fallen so hard for. The guy from San Francisco.

No wonder, Amy thought as she felt her heart begin to beat in heavy strokes. *No wonder our connection was so strong.* She'd already been dreaming of him, day and night.

Other **ENCHANTED HEARTS** Books
from Avon Flare

#1: THE HAUNTED HEART
by Cherie Bennett

#2: ETERNALLY YOURS
by Jennifer Baker

Coming Soon

#4: LOVE POTION
by Janet Quin-Harkin

#5: SPELLBOUND
by Phyllis Karas

#6: LOVE HIM FOREVER
by Cherie Bennett

enchanted ❤3 HEARTS

Lost and Found

Cameron Dokey

AN AVON FLARE BOOK

AVON BOOKS, INC.
1350 Avenue of the Americas
New York, New York 10019

Copyright © 1999 by Mary Cameron Dokey
Excerpt from *Love Potion* copyright © 1999 by Janet Quin-Harkin
Published by arrangement with the author
Library of Congress Catalog Card Number: 98-94856
ISBN: 0-380-80083-7
www.avonbooks.com

First Avon Flare Printing: August 1999

AVON FLARE TRADEMARK REG. U.S. PAT. OFF. AND IN OTHER COUNTRIES, MARCA REGISTRADA, HECHO EN U.S.A.

Printed in the U.S.A.

WCD 10 9 8 7 6 5 4 3 2 1

For the wonderful editor I ''found'' while
writing this book,
Abigail McAden

Lost and
Found

one
1

He was gone, and she would never find him again.

Amy Johnson sat at her bedroom window, her palms resting on the open sketchbook in her lap.

On the face she'd sketched just that morning. Hoping against hope that this time it would be different. That this sketch would be the one to help her beat the odds she knew were stacked against her.

That it would be the one to help her call him back.

Usually, the view from her bedroom window was Amy's favorite thing in the whole world. But today she hardly registered it.

She didn't notice the white sails of the boats skimming across sparkling blue water. The summer day's picture postcard perfection. Didn't see her own image, short brown hair, heart-shaped face, eyes the same color as the water, reflected in the windowpane.

Instead, her eyes saw what her mind saw. A thick gray emptiness. *Like the surface of the moon,* Amy thought. *Which is where I might as well be.*

She had to face the fact that she was never going to find him. The guy she'd met just once but seemed unable to forget. The only guy who'd ever made her heart race, just with a smile. She could still remember the way surprise had lit his eyes when she'd smiled back.

But now he was two thousand miles away. Out of reach. And so was her best chance for true love.

"*Amy?*"

Amy started, her head jerking forward to crack against the window frame. With one hand, she reached to rub her smarting forehead. With the other, she quickly closed the sketchbook and thrust it behind the back cushion of the window seat.

She didn't want her father to see the sketchbook or the portraits in it. She didn't want him to guess what she'd been doing. That she'd been trying to reactivate her talent, get it to work again. It would only worry him if he knew. And it would cause her mother to have an absolute fit.

Amy turned as she heard the door *snick* open. A moment later, her father's face peered around it. *Not quite in. Not quite out,* Amy thought with a flash of irritation. *The safe approach.*

"Dad," she said.

Even to her own ears, her voice sounded whiny. Amy hated it when she sounded like a baby. She could take care of herself, and she shouldn't have to keep on proving it.

"I thought we had an agreement," she went on, her tone more aggressive. "When my door is closed, you have to knock. You can't just barge right in. Now you've probably given me a black eye or something."

"I have been knocking, Amy," her father answered. He stepped all the way into the room but left the door ajar behind him.

"I knocked for a long time, in fact. Long enough for me to decide I'd better break our agreement to check and see if you were all right."

Amy felt a chill shoot through her.

It had been months since she'd heard her father use that careful tone of voice. Long enough so that she'd hoped the need for it had gone for good.

"I don't need you to check on me, Dad," she said, her voice sharp. "I'm not in here having a nervous breakdown."

Another one.

"I didn't say I thought you were," her father said.

Amy could feel his eyes on her. She looked up to meet them. They were the exact same color as her own. A vivid, multilayered blue. Deep ocean.

But there were dark shadows under her father's blue eyes. Shadows Amy knew she'd given him. Knew because they matched the ones she'd given herself.

Looking at her father's worried face, Amy felt her chill vanish as a wave of guilt washed over her.

Her parents had done everything they could to help her get over all the things that had happened the previous year in San Francisco. All the things that had finally been too much for her. They'd changed their whole lives.

Changed states, moving from California to Washington. Her mom had closed her thriving art gallery and was struggling to reestablish it. Her dad had gone from being a big-city detective to being a small-town one.

Her parents had even waited to buy a new house until they'd found the perfect one for Amy, one where she could see the water from her bedroom window, because the water soothed her somehow. Made even the nightmares easier.

They'd given up everything. Torn apart their whole lives. All so Amy could have a chance to start again. To heal. And how was she paying them back? By being a jerk.

"I'm sorry, Dad," she got out, dismayed to find her voice choked with tears. "It's just—" Amy broke off, her throat too thick to continue.

It's just what? she thought. *It's just I was always*

3

so sure I'd be so happy if I woke up one morning to find that I could be the thing I'd always dreamed about but never was? Normal, not a freak. Not "Oh, you're that Amy Johnson."

Only now that I think it's finally happened, I can't handle it. Because it isn't what I really wanted after all?

Her father moved to sit beside her on the window seat. "Disturbance in the Force, huh?" he asked.

Amy made a watery sound.

It was an old joke between them. Almost as old as their discovery of what they referred to as her talent. The thing that made her so different from everybody else. That had set her apart, even when she was small.

That had deprived her of childhood birthday parties, because the thing that she could do frightened the other kids' parents. Of dates when she'd grown older, because no guy wanted to go out with a girl who could read his mind.

It hadn't done any good to explain that her talent didn't work that way. That she couldn't really read minds. Other people thought she could, and that was all that counted.

Except to her father, who'd told her she was like Luke Skywalker. That she was part of the Force. Her dad was the one who'd made her feel good about the strange thing she could do, Amy realized. The *only* one.

Amy was dismayed to feel her tears begin to slip silently down her cheeks.

"Hey now," her father said. "Take it easy, sport."

Amy reached up to wipe her wet cheeks. "Oh, Dad. I'm sorry."

"What's to be sorry about?" her father asked. "I've seen tears before. Manly men aren't afraid of a woman's tears," he continued, as if sharing secret knowledge.

4

He produced a large, white cotton handkerchief and held it up to Amy's face. "Here," he said. "Now blow."

Obediently, Amy blew her nose. She felt totally ridiculous, and incredibly better, all at the same time.

"I can do it myself, you know," she protested. "I'm not a baby."

"Are too," her father said.

"Am not."

"Booger face."

"Snot nose."

Amy could feel the grin starting to work its way from the corners of her mouth across the rest of her features.

She knew if she looked into her father's eyes the concern she'd shied away from earlier would be gone and they would be filled with laughter. She loved it when her father laughed. Hated it when he had to stop.

"Mucus man."

"Goober girl."

"Loogie Louie."

"Loogie *Louise*."

"Hey," Amy protested at once. "You stole mine. That's no fair. You can't do that."

"I'm your father," Stan Johnson answered. "I can do anything."

Impulsively, Amy threw her arms around his neck and buried her face against his shoulder. He'd made her feel better when she'd thought nothing could. He was right. He *could* do anything.

She felt her father's strong arms wrap around her, holding her close. And safe. And warm. Just like always.

"So," Stan Johnson said softly, "you want to tell me what this is all about, sport?"

Oh, Dad, Amy thought. *I can't.*

5

She'd never told her parents about the one good thing that had happened those last days in California. A thing so unexpected, so remarkable and wonderful even in the midst of all the horror, Amy had almost begged her parents to give up their moving plans.

But how could she explain that she couldn't leave San Francisco—couldn't leave the scene of nightmares so vivid she woke up screaming—because moving to Washington meant she'd lose her only chance of being with a guy she'd met only once and might never see again?

A guy whose name she didn't even know but whom Amy was absolutely positive was her true love. Her soul mate.

She couldn't. She couldn't even imagine attempting to explain that she'd fallen in love over something as simple as a conversation about ordinary things.

Other people had conversations like that all the time. Whether or not their sports teams had won. What their favorite flavor of ice cream was. But not Amy. Never Amy.

And then the chance meeting had ended as suddenly as it had started, shattered by the reality of her situation. She'd never told her parents about it, what it had meant to her to spend even a moment with someone who didn't know who she was and so had no expectations. None that didn't arise from what they could create together.

No, she'd never told her parents how much that simple thing had meant to her. And now it was too late to say anything.

"No, I don't want to tell you what this is all about, sport," she answered.

Her father laughed under his breath, as if he wasn't quite ready to admit that she'd amused him.

Amy's mother hated her sarcasm. She called it an unhealthy defense mechanism. But it never seemed to bother her father. He always knew how to come right back. Her mom had also never agreed with Amy's decision to use her talent.

"Not the answer I was hoping for," Stan Johnson admitted now with a shake of his head. His blue eyes watched Amy for just a moment, as if trying to decide whether or not to push the issue. "But I guess it's one that I can live with."

Amy felt a surge of gratitude. Even when her father was worried, he trusted her. She sat up straight. Her father's arms fell away. But Amy swore she could still feel their support.

"I got Funny One out today."

Amy saw her father's eyes widen as they flickered over her shoulder to stare at the stuffed clown on her bed. Funny One.

"So you did," Stan Johnson commented.

The neutral voice was back in place again, Amy noted. But this time it didn't bother her. She could almost hear her father playing twenty questions inside his head.

Was the reappearance of Funny One a good development or a bad one? A move forward or a move back?

"He looks pretty good for an old guy."

"He's younger than you."

"Ouch," her father said.

Amy twisted around so that she, too, could look at the stuffed clown leaning up against her pillows. Over the years, his original vivid yellow-and-white coloring had faded to a uniform gray.

But Funny One was the only thing Amy had brought with her to her new home. The only memento she'd wanted from her past.

She'd kept him packed away until today, though. He had too many associations she wasn't sure she was ready to face. Because Funny One had been the start

7

of everything. Holding him, the first proof that she was different.

Looking at him now, Amy felt something deep inside her shift. Felt her perception sharpen, as if some unseen hand had touched the knob that played back the images of the day and brought them into sudden focus. Perfect sense.

She saw again the boats on the water. Her own face reflected in the glass. And then a flash of light she hadn't registered before. Glancing from the windshield of the car she didn't recognize, backing out of her own driveway.

"There was someone here, wasn't there?" she asked. Behind her, she heard her father catch and hold his breath.

"I heard you and Mom talking to him, then you guys arguing. That's why I closed my door in the first place."

So she wouldn't have to hear the sound of her mother's voice. The panic in it. The anger and the pain. There was only one thing that made her mother sound like that.

Fear. Fear for Amy.

"He was a cop, wasn't he?" Amy guessed. "But not from here. You didn't know him. He was a stranger."

At long last, she heard her father expel his pent-up breath. "He was from Seattle," he answered. "Something happened there today. Something like—"

He broke off, and Amy heard him rub his hand across his face. It made a scratchy sound, the way it usually did. Her father had a five o'clock shadow by ten in the morning.

And he always rubbed his face when he was thinking something he didn't quite know how to say.

But Amy knew what it was. Knew her father didn't need to say it.

"He wants to see me, doesn't he?" she said.

two

"You don't have to say yes."

At the sound of the new voice, both Amy and her father swiveled toward the doorway.

Amy's mother had pushed the door completely open and now stood in front of it, as if blocking the only means of escape. Her face was tight with emotion, fear, and anger battling for supremacy.

Amy felt an ache start, low and dull, at the back of her head. She hated it that her parents argued about whether or not she should use her talent. That they'd always argued about it.

"Gee, Mom, come on in. Don't bother to knock," she said.

"You don't have to say yes," Rebecca Johnson repeated through tight lips. But she wasn't talking to Amy. She wasn't even looking in her direction. All her energy was focused on her husband. She glared at him now, her hands on her hips, her brown eyes furious.

"Your mother and I didn't agree on whether or not I should bring this matter to your attention," her father explained quietly.

"No kidding, really?" Amy said.

Once again, her mother ignored her. "That man, that—" Rebecca Johnson sputtered.

"Detective Carlson," her husband filled in.

"Detective Carlson." Amy's mother pounced on the name. "He has no business coming here. No business asking us to do this."

He's not asking you, Mom, Amy thought. *He's asking me.*

If there'd ever been a time when her parents hadn't disagreed about whether or not Amy should use her talent, she couldn't remember it. They'd been over this ground so often Amy was sure she knew just what her dad would say next.

"He has a case to solve," Stan Johnson answered. "It's perfectly reasonable for him to explore every avenue, including this one."

Amy made one last-ditch effort to break the deadlock between her parents.

"Gee, Dad, I love it when you sound like *Law and Order.*"

But her mother rode right over her. "And you just let him in," Rebecca Johnson said. "Into this house, which was supposed to be your daughter's safe haven. You know better than anyone how hard that kind of work is on her. How it leaves her worn out, depressed, exhausted.

"But all some *fellow officer* has to do is knock at the door and you throw it wide open. You run the risk of destroying everything we've worked so hard for, all for some misguided notion of cop solidarity. But Amy does not have to be a part of this, Stan. She does not have to say yes."

Amy could almost feel the exact second her father lost his temper. "She knows she doesn't have to say yes," Stan Johnson all but shouted as he surged up from the window seat. "That's her decision, just the way it's always been. I have never forced Amy to participate in any case she didn't want to."

Amy felt her headache sharpen. Blossom.

"We agreed, we *both* agreed, it was time to find out the truth about what was happening with Amy's talent," her father continued. "If it's gone, then Carlson's visit will be over quickly."

"And if it isn't?" Amy's mother asked.

"If it isn't, then whether or not she works this case is up to Amy, just like always," her husband answered. "I don't want her hurt or worn out or frightened any more than you do, Rebecca. But this may be our best opportunity to find out if she's really lost her talent. The fact that you don't like it doesn't change the situation. So stop trying to make me out to be the bad guy here."

"Thanks so much for deciding what was best for me," Amy put in. "When were you thinking of telling me about it?"

There was a startled silence as both parents turned to stare at her. Almost like they'd forgotten her existence, Amy thought. Which they probably had. Otherwise, they never would have let slip the fact that they'd been discussing her.

Amy knew all parents discussed their children, but it still felt an awful lot like her parents had decided something behind her back. Amy wanted to feel angry about it. But she couldn't.

The trouble was, she agreed with them.

It *was* time to discover what was happening with her talent. Or wasn't happening with it. She just wished her parents had let her in on the discussion a little earlier. And not in the middle of one of their arguments.

Through the window seat cushion, Amy could feel the sharp edge of her sketchbook digging into her ribs.

Well, she thought, *I guess we're even.*

Her parents had come to a conclusion they hadn't shared with her. She had a secret she hadn't shared with them. And none of it made a difference if her talent really was gone, as she was afraid it was.

"Is somebody going to tell me what's going on or not?" she asked. In the silence her words caused, Amy saw the anger drain from her mother's face until only the fear was left.

I'm sorry, Mom, she thought. *But you've never really understood why I have to do this.*

"Go on, Stan," Rebecca Johnson said. "You might as well get it over with."

Her father ran his hand across his face once more.

"There's been a kidnapping, Amy," he said.

Amy felt a rush of adrenaline even as her gut clenched. *A kidnapping. I should have known,* she thought. *It always comes back to that.*

No longer able to sit still, she got up from the window seat and crossed to the bed. Funny One lay against the pillows, his button eyes the only things still bright and shiny about him.

What would her life have been like if Funny One had never come into it? Amy wondered. Would it ever have been normal? Or was it always just a matter of time until the incidents began?

That's what one of the paranormal specialists her parents had taken her to later had called them. Incidents of clairvoyance. Though even the doctor who claimed to be an expert in such matters had never seen a talent like Amy had.

A talent that put her inside a victim's head.

The first incident had happened when Amy was only six. When she'd still been blissfully unaware that anything about her would ever be different. When she'd hardly even been aware what being different meant. But all that changed the day her best friend, Kara Taylor, went to school. As usual.

Unlike usual, she didn't come back.

It was Kara's mother who came to tell them Kara had been kidnapped. A slew of police officers already in tow, Audrey Taylor had descended on the Johnson house like a hurricane.

She didn't care if the officers with her were some of the best in San Francisco. She wanted Detective Stan Johnson on the case. She already knew and trusted him. As far as Audrey Taylor was concerned, her daughter's life was in Stan Johnson's hands.

But Kara's mother had been clutching something in her own trembling hands. The stuffed clown that Kara loved so much she even took it to school with her, the token the kidnapper had sent along with the ransom demands.

Audrey hadn't noticed when Stan had coaxed the clown from her fingers and set it on the kitchen table. Neither of them had noticed when it tumbled to the floor.

And nobody at all had noticed when young Amy trailed her father into the kitchen. Bent over and picked up the forgotten toy. Nobody'd noticed when her body had begun to shake and her eyes grew blank and wide.

They'd noticed when she'd started to scream, though.

Scream that Kara was in a strange place. A place that frightened her. With a man who frightened her.

Scream that Amy knew where Kara was.

Her father had knelt in front of her then and put his strong, gentle hands on her shoulders. He would find her friend, he promised. That was his job. But he would do it faster if Amy would calm down.

Now was not the time to tell him stories, her father continued. She told good stories, and he liked to hear them. But he didn't have time to listen right now.

Right now what Amy could do to help was to make sure that Funny One was safe. Would Amy take the clown up to her room and have him lie down?

I can't do that, Papa, Amy had answered. *I need to hold him so I can see the pictures.*

What pictures, Amy? her father had asked, his patient voice strained almost to the breaking point.

The pictures from Kara.

Even now, ten years later, Amy still didn't know what her father had seen in her face. What he'd heard in her voice that had made him change his mind. That had made him believe her. Believe she knew something it made no sense for her to know. And ask her to go on.

She only knew he had. And that, finally, the whole kitchen full of grown-ups had fallen silent as she'd described the pictures she was seeing. The ones she was so certain were what Kara was seeing. That showed her where Kara was.

They'd faded over the years, of course. But sometimes Amy swore she could still see them when she looked into Funny One's white button eyes.

The room shrouded in the heavy curtains decorated with blood-red flowers that had so frightened Kara. The room that had made her sick to her stomach with its grandmother smell.

And then Amy's voice had been silenced by the ringing of the phone. The police lab had a match for the handwriting on the ransom note. The kidnapper was a former employee of Kara's father's, fired just the month before.

"He grew up in Oakland," the uniformed officer who'd answered the phone told Amy's father in a low voice. "His mother lived there until last month. He put her in a nursing home the same day he was fired."

Amy had never forgotten the way her father's eyes had searched her upturned face. Then he had turned from her and answered, "Go. No sirens. If you see curtains that match my daughter's description, go in there first."

Two hours later the police brought Kara home alive and safe. Because of the pictures only Amy Johnson had been able to see. Because of her strange talent.

The press had had a field day when word of her involvement leaked out. PSYCHIC TYKE SAVES BEST FRIEND, the headlines had proclaimed. Television crews from all over the country had camped in front of the house for a solid week.

From that moment on, Amy had known that she was different. And she'd known that nothing in her life would ever be the same.

The Taylors had divorced not long after that. Kara's mother had taken Kara away. But before she left, Kara had performed one final act of friendship.

She'd given Funny One to Amy.

Amy never saw any more pictures when she held him. Once Kara was safe, Funny One was just a toy again. As the years went by, Amy had fallen asleep with her arms wrapped around him more times than she could count.

It became more and more clear that Amy's special talent, wherever it came from, lay in finding people— particularly young people—nobody else could find. She'd continued to work missing person cases with the police—over her mother's vehement objections but with her father's quiet support.

The images her talent conjured up became more and more terrifying as time went on. Harder and harder to wipe from her mind, even with the comfort of her arms around Funny One.

Until the day one image became so horrible, seared into her brain by an act of desperation so senseless, Amy's mind had rebelled and her talent had simply shut down.

In all the years, it was the only image she'd ever run from. They'd all run from it. Her whole family. All the way from California to Washington.

And now a Washington cop had come to her house. And the cycle was about to start all over again.

But not in my room, Amy thought. *Not in the one place that's truly mine.*

She picked up Funny One, cradling him in her arms gently. "How many?" she asked, turning to face her father.

Her mother made a low, distressed sound.

"Just one," her dad said.

"Not in here," Amy answered.

Her father nodded. "Living room okay?" he asked.

This time, it was Amy who nodded. "What'd you do, tell him to drive around for half an hour?"

Her father shrugged. "I sent him to the nearest Starbucks."

"Double tall mocha, extra whip."

"Gotcha," her dad said.

"Unbelievable," Amy's mother muttered. "I am totally opposed to this. I want you both to know that." She threw up her hands and stomped off.

Amy made silent eye contact with her father. Her mom never understood why she continued to say yes, time after time. Even now, when she wasn't sure saying yes would do any good anymore.

But her dad knew. He'd known from the moment he'd first decided to believe her all those years ago.

She said yes because she had to. Because she didn't have a choice.

Amy turned back to the bed and tucked Funny One protectively in among the pillows. He wasn't a part of her talent anymore.

She was about to discover if she still was.

Trying to ignore the heavy pounding of her heart, Amy walked into the living room and listened to her father place the call to Detective Carlson.

three
3

"*The victim's name is Nicholas Granger,*" said Detective Carlson. "Caucasian male, seventeen years of age. His father is the wealthy industrialist Elmore Granger."

"Never heard of him," Amy's father said. He always sat in on her meetings with the police. If the situation turned out to be one Amy could help with, then her father worked with her, assigned to the case.

At the moment, though, he was just keeping the ball rolling. So far, Amy hadn't said a thing. That didn't seem to bother Detective Carlson. He was more than happy talking to Amy's father.

He nodded now in response to Stan Johnson's comment. "That's not surprising," he answered. "Granger Senior is almost a total recluse. As far as we know, nobody's seen him for years. We didn't even know he'd moved to this area."

"So that's why the son was taken?" Stan Johnson asked. "For the father's money?"

The Seattle policeman shrugged. "Could be."

But you don't think so, Amy thought.

She could already tell the interview was going to be about as much fun as pulling teeth. If Detective Carlson was there because he wanted to be, Amy'd eat the coffee table.

17

She pried the top off her mocha and got the detective's full attention. She could feel his eyes on her. Watching. Waiting for her to exhibit some sign of her strange talent. They all did that at first. Treated her like she was some bizarre science experiment. As if at any moment she might start foaming at the mouth. Grow fangs and extra hair.

You could use a little extra hair yourself, Detective, Amy thought.

With the exception of his head, which was round as a cue ball, the Seattle detective was built big and square. Like a Volvo, Amy thought. His eyes were slate gray, like the water on a cloudy winter morning.

A Volvo fuming at a stoplight, Amy ammended, watching him. Who was afraid he was going to run out of gas in the bargain. It didn't take a clairvoyant to figure out that Volvo Carlson wanted to be somewhere else. Anywhere else.

Amy dropped the plastic lid onto the saucer her mom had brought in from the kitchen before stomping back out again.

She didn't really want to drink the chocolate-flavored coffee, but the ritual of it would help her focus. With luck, it would also keep the detective from noticing that her hands were shaking.

She took a sip of coffee, wiped whipped cream from her lip. "What's the time line?" she asked.

"Seventy-two hours," the detective answered.

Amy felt a spurt of surprise. "Three days? Isn't that awfully long? If Nick's dad is so rich, he ought to be able to put the money together a lot faster than that."

Detective Carlson pursed his lips. "Maybe," he said.

And that's why you think this kidnapping isn't about Nick's father's money, Amy realized. *Though you'd rather be boiled in oil than tell me that.*

"What does he look like?" she asked.

"Who, Elmore Granger?"

"No, his son."

"I thought you were supposed to tell me," the detective countered.

Great, Amy thought. *Here we go.*

Detective Carlson was what Amy called a tester. He wouldn't accept her because he'd been asked to, or even on the basis of her previous successes. He'd only trust her when she'd proved herself to him.

Amy supposed his point of view wasn't unreasonable. The trouble was, testers always brought out the worst in her. She always wanted to test them back.

"Sorry, it doesn't work that way, Detective."

"How does 'it' work?" the Volvo said.

"Now wait just a minute—" Amy's father interrupted.

Amy cut him off quickly. "It's okay, Dad," she said. "The detective and I have never worked together before. It's a legitimate question."

She leaned forward. " 'It' works like this, Detective," she said. "Sometimes, when I handle an object, I get impressions of the person who owns it. I can get inside the person's head. See through his or her eyes. It's why the police use me for cases like this. Because I see what the victim sees."

"But it doesn't happen every time you touch something," the detective put in, skepticism thick in his voice. "Only sometimes."

"That's right," Amy said. "If you were to hand me your notebook, for instance, I don't think it would help me get inside your head. My talent works best in situations where the owner of the object is under extreme emotional distress."

"But that doesn't make any sense," Detective Carlson objected. "It should work every time you touch something, shouldn't it?"

"I only said I know the way it works," Amy answered. "I never said I know why it works the way it does."

Detective Carlson let out a sigh.

"Look, I'm sorry," the big man said. "I don't mean to offend you or your father, Miss Johnson. But I think you should know I argued with my lieutenant for a solid hour about making this trip. As far as I'm concerned, what we're doing here is a big a waste of time."

"That's okay. You may be right," Amy admitted. "But it looks like you lost that long argument, Detective. How come?"

The detective looked straight into her eyes.

Amy'd seen the look before, on the faces of other testers. It was the one that said "Okay, little girl, you asked for it."

"The lieutenant grew up in San Francisco. His nephew was one of the kids taken by the Rising Dawn."

Amy jerked. A wave of hot coffee cascaded onto her lap. She was sure her father cried out. But Amy couldn't hear it over the roaring in her ears.

I'll never be free, she thought. *No matter where I go, no matter what I do.*

Her mother had been wrong. This house wasn't a safe haven. There was no such thing as a safe haven for her. The terrifying sequence of events of a year before in San Francisco would follow her wherever she went.

Twenty-five second graders held hostage by a doomsday cult. Amy had helped rescue twenty-four of them. Had found them deep within the cult compound when no one else could. Saving precious hours. Precious lives.

Twenty-four terrified children snatched from the

jaws of death. All except the one who haunted Amy's dreams.

The one who didn't make it out in time.

When the cultists discovered the police had penetrated their defenses, they'd set fire to their own compound. Too terrified to follow his classmates to safety, the last hostage, one small boy, had perished with the cult members.

For months afterward, Amy had seen the images, *his* last images, every single time she closed her eyes.

The dark room of his captivity. Suddenly illuminated by a horrible, flickering light. A light that grew brighter. Closer. Hotter. Roaring as it devoured everything before it.

Until the boy had done the thing that haunted Amy's dreams. That never left her, day or night. The only thing left for him to do.

He'd lifted his hands to cover his eyes.

Amy hadn't been able to see after that. But she'd been able to fight. Her father told her later she'd fought so hard it had taken four large policemen to hold her. Four grown men to prevent her from going after that last small boy herself.

"Not Brian Newcomb, I assume," she said, amazed to hear her voice come out all right.

It was the first time she'd said his name in almost a year. The name of the only hostage she hadn't been able to save. Her only failure. And the cause of her greatest fear.

Fear that—if her talent had survived—she was doomed to fail from now on. That's how long she'd see Brian Newcomb's face in her nightmares.

Detective Carlson shifted as if the chair had suddenly grown too small for him.

"Not Brian Newcomb, no," he answered. "The lieutenant's nephew was one of the ones who—"

21

"One of the lucky ones," Amy interrupted. "One of the ones who got away."

"I'm sorry," Detective Carlson said.

He reached into the Starbucks bag that had once held Amy's coffee and handed her a wad of paper napkins.

"Can you help me find Nick Granger?" he asked.

Amy blotted her lap.

This was it. The moment of truth. The one her whole family longed for but had been so carefully avoiding.

"I genuinely don't know, Detective," she answered. "If you know about Rising Dawn, you probably know I wasn't very . . . well . . . afterwards."

Amy tossed the soggy napkins onto the coffee table.

"I had a nervous breakdown," she said baldly. "It's why my family moved up here. I haven't tried to use my talent since—in nearly a year. I don't even know if I *can* use it. If I still have it."

"Is there a way you can find out?" Carlson asked.

There was a beat of silence. Amy stared at the coffee stains on her lap. "I'd have to try to use it," she admitted.

And realized she was really going to do it. Get involved again. Risk another failure. But if she failed this time, she wasn't sure she could ever come back.

In the silence, Amy could hear the clock, ticking on the mantel. Abruptly, she realized all three occupants of the living room were holding their breath. She released hers first.

"I'll need objects—things that belonged to Nick Granger. The more important they were to him, the more contact he had with them, the better. And the person who brings them to me should handle them as little as possible."

Detective Carlson expelled air, his mouth pursed in

a silent whistle as he whipped open his notebook and jotted down Amy's comments.

"Got it."

Amy heard her father's chair creak as he shifted position. She understood his nonverbal signal.

"My father is always a part of the team when I work a case," she continued.

"That's all been cleared," the detective said.

Amy felt a sudden chill sweep over her. Somebody had been awfully sure that she'd say yes. She could feel the fear rising up to choke her. What would happen if she failed again? To her—and to Nick Granger?

"All I'm promising is that I'll try," she said. "I'm not sure I can even do this anymore. If I can't—" Amy looked at her dad. *I learn to live my life over again,* she thought.

"If I can't, I stop. That's the end of it. I'm taken off this case, and nobody asks me to work another one. Ever."

Her father cleared his throat before he spoke.

"I understand."

Amy switched her attention to Detective Carlson.

"Understood," he said. "I'll rely on you to let me know if you've, um, made contact."

For the first time that afternoon, Amy laughed.

"Believe me, Detective, if this works, you won't need me to tell you if I've made contact."

"Okay, whatever," the detective said. He still looked uncomfortable, but now Amy was pretty sure they both could handle it.

"Would it be all right if I called you by your first name, Detective?" she asked.

"Call me Carl like everybody else does," the detective said. He smiled, directly at Amy this time. She smiled back.

"Time is a factor, so if there's nothing else, I should call the father," Carl said.

"There's a phone in the kitchen," Amy's father broke his long silence. "Just around the corner there."

Detective Carlson got up to use the telephone. Amy's father waited until the other man was in the other room before he spoke again.

"You're sure?" he asked.

"No," Amy answered. "But he's right. *You're* right," she said. "I have to know, one way or the other."

If only she could decide which answer would be worse.

four
𝒟

He was trapped.

In the dark, in a place he wasn't sure he could bring himself to think about. Because he was sure he wouldn't be able to stop himself from screaming if he did. A place so terrible, nothing in any nightmare could touch it.

The place from which there was no escape. The place in which he'd wake up dead.

He could feel it, close along both sides of his body. He kicked the top of it if he moved his feet. It left him barely enough room to slide his arms up his chest crossways so that he could press his hands above his face.

Wood. Smooth and smelling strongly of something. Something much more potent than paint.

It was a smell that reminded him of the time he'd helped his friend Pat fix up Pat's family's back deck. They'd stained it with something. Something to make the wood repel water. To make it waterproof.

Waterproof.

He did scream, then.

Until his throat was raw and hoarse and then went dead. Until his screaming ceased to make a sound. And the dark was filled with hot, white spots that danced in front of his streaming eyes.

Oh, God. Oh, please, God, no. Don't let it be that.

25

five

5

"*Thank you for agreeing to do this, Miss Johnson,*" Elmore Granger said. "I don't imagine it can be very pleasant."

With his back to the late-afternoon sun, it was hard for Amy to see his face, but he had one of the most compelling voices she had ever heard. Deep and melodic.

A bedtime story voice, Amy thought, and wondered how many times the man opposite her had used his beautiful voice to comfort his son as he read him to sleep.

"Please call me Amy, Mr. Granger," she answered. "And, please, don't worry about me."

The answer started as polite reflex, but by the time she was finished speaking Amy was surprised to discover that she meant it. The truth was, she liked Nick Granger's father. He was nothing like what she'd expected.

The words "wealthy industrialist" had conjured up visions of someone ruthless in a business suit. Someone who could compel or repel on sight, someone along the lines of the *X-Files*'s Cigarette-Smoking Man.

But Elmore Granger looked more like a candidate for a mall Santa Claus. He was slightly older than

Amy's own father. His close-cropped hair was turning white. He wasn't round. But there was something reassuring about him. Something that invited shared confidences.

At the moment, it was hard for Amy to see his features clearly, since he'd chosen a chair in shadow and Amy faced the sun. But she was sure Elmore Granger's eyes were on her. Watching. Waiting for her to set the pace.

Amy glanced at her father, seated beside her on the couch since he'd given up his seat to their guest. Her dad always stayed physically close when Amy worked.

Her father nodded encouragingly. Out of the corner of her eye, Amy could see Detective Carlson, who'd been prowling the outskirts of the room, stop and mimic her father's action.

Okay, she thought. *Let's get this over with.*

"Might I see the objects?" she asked.

"Of course," said Elmore Granger.

He turned his head. Immediately, his assistant, Steve Dorsey, stepped forward. In his arms, he cradled a cardboard box. He set it on the coffee table in front of Amy. She avoided looking at him. Elmore Granger might have been a surprise, but his assistant wasn't.

Mid-twenties. Dark hair. Green eyes that were startling in their color and intensity. His square-chinned good looks made him look like a model for the J. Crew catalog. Except he was wearing a three-piece suit.

If there was a person in the room who fit Amy's preconceived notions of what a ruthless tycoon was like, Steve Dorsey was it. Any more hard-edged and Amy was sure she could cut paper on him. Assuming she didn't cut herself first.

She yanked her attention back to the box.

Come on, Amy. Stop procrastinating.

"Is there anything here that's particularly important to your son?" she asked.

There was a beat of silence.

"I'm sorry. I—I don't know," said Elmore Granger.

Surprise showed in Amy's face before she could stop it.

"Please, allow me to explain," the elder Granger said. "Nick's mother and I divorced when he was very young. After the divorce, my ex-wife and I were totally estranged.

"Nick's childhood was spent with his mother. She died some years ago, but by then Nick was old enough to be at boarding school. It was an act of cowardice, perhaps, but I allowed him to remain there until he graduated.

"After that, however, I decided I wanted the situation to change. Perhaps it's the fact that I'm growing older, but . . . I wanted Nick to live with me. For us to have a chance to start again. To get to know each other. In time, I hoped we could become a real family."

Elmore Granger's voice faltered.

"Nick is my only son," he said. "My only child. The only family I will ever have. I moved us here so we could learn to be together. But now—with this—"

He broke off. For the first time, Amy was glad his face was in the shadows. That way, she couldn't see if there were tears in his eyes.

Brian Newcomb's parents had cried when she couldn't save him.

"I'll just start, then, and see what happens," Amy said.

And wished she could bring herself to say "Don't worry, Mr. Granger. I'm sure we'll find him."

A year ago, she might have done it. Now she had

no comfort to give. Not when there was such a good chance it would be false comfort. Cold comfort.

Trying to ignore the pounding of her heart, Amy reached into the cardboard box and pulled out a shiny ballpoint pen.

Cool metal. Smooth against her fingers. Amy closed her eyes and gripped the pen as if she were about to write a composition. It felt easy in her hand. Right.

I'd save it for something special, Amy thought, if this pen were mine. Something like journal writing. An important ritual she'd perform every day.

But Nicholas Granger hadn't felt that way about it. Either that or Amy's talent truly was gone. Because the pen was just a pen. It conjured up no images. Told her absolutely nothing about its owner. Didn't show her where he was.

Amy's heart began to pound a little faster. A little harder. Like the beating of a stopwatch. Counting down to the moment when Nick Granger would be lost forever.

In less than three days now. Fewer than seventy-two hours. And every moment Amy hesitated, every object she touched that told her nothing, only brought them closer to that moment.

Heart kicking against her ribs, Amy opened her eyes and set the pen down on the coffee table.

"Nothing," she said, though she knew she didn't need to. And reached into the box again.

The coffee table was soon littered with objects discarded from the box, and Amy's palms were sweating. Now her heartbeats thundered in her ears in a fast, uneven rhythm.

The silence in the room crowded down upon her. It was so thick, Amy could have carved it and served it on a plate like a Thanksgiving turkey. The ridiculous image made her feel giddy. Light-headed. *Steady,* she told herself. *I've got to say something. Do something.*

But how could she tell the silent man across from her his son was lost because she'd lost her only means to find him?

Out of the corner of her eye, she saw her mother watching her from the shadowy hallway.

Amy cleared her throat. "Detective Carlson did explain, didn't he?" she asked. Even to her own ears, her voice sounded exhausted. As if she'd been speaking for hours and hours. Trying to explain something for which there was no explanation.

"He told you I might not be able to do this?"

Elmore Granger shifted in his chair, leaning forward so that, for the first time since he'd arrived, Amy could see him clearly.

He looks so sad, she thought. His rich, dark eyes, so like his voice, were filled with shadows.

"The detective said you had been having—difficulties," Elmore Granger answered. "I knew this was a long shot, Amy. I wanted to try everything, though." He paused, his eyes kindling as he looked into her face.

"Is that the end, then? Is that everything?"

Amy looked inside the box. "No," she answered. "There's one more thing."

Something she hadn't seen until now. Hidden in the corner of the box beneath a hardback book Nick hadn't been reading.

A watch. The expensive kind your grandparents gave you for graduation. Though Nick Granger could probably afford a different one for every day of the week.

It probably meant no more to him than any of the other things she'd touched, Amy thought.

Now all she had to do was to touch the watch and

it would all be over. *How long will it take me to get used to being normal?* she wondered.

Amy felt her fingers close around the watch face.

It was like she'd taken a bolt of lightning straight to the head.

Amy's whole body spasmed, hurling her backward. Elbows tight against her body, legs shooting out straight. The coffee table crashed over as her feet hit it, but she never even noticed. Her hands beat the air above her face.

Breathe, she thought. *I can't breathe. I'm going to die in this terrible place.*

From a great distance, she heard someone begin to gasp for breath. The sound was thick. And loud. And desperate.

Oh, God, she thought. *That's me. That's* Nick.

In the next instant, she felt someone try to pry the watch from her fingers. "No," Amy screamed.

"Amy, let go," her father said. "Give me the watch. *Give it to me, Amy.*"

Amy struggled for control, trying to beat the panic back. The watch clenched tightly in one fist.

She took one breath. Then another. And another. The terrible pressure in her chest began to ease. Abruptly, she realized the gasping had stopped.

"Don't, Dad," she managed to say as she felt her father's fingers close around the watch. "Let me. I can do this."

Her father made a sound of frustration and denial. Amy thought she heard her mother's sharp voice say "Amy!" But it was Detective Carlson's voice that finally made sense.

"All right, Amy," he said, steady as a rock. "I take it this means you've made contact."

"I told you so," she managed.

"That's right, you did," Detective Carlson answered. "Now I want you to really impress me. Concentrate, Amy. Tell me what you—and Nick—can see."

six

6

"*I*t's dark," Amy said, and fought the impulse to laugh hysterically. "We can't see a thing."

"All right," Detective Carlson said once more. "What about other sensations? Can you hear something? Smell something? Can you feel anything?"

This time, Amy did laugh. Though she could feel the taste of panic rising sour in the back of her throat. The detective moved to crouch on her other side, so that Amy was between him and her father.

"Come on, Amy," Detective Carlson said. "Stay with me on this. Can you identify where Nick is?"

Amy closed her eyes. It was easier to concentrate that way. But with her eyes shut, it was also easier to feel the tightness, the *smallness* of the thing that held Nick Granger.

Amy's throat began to ache with the effort she was making to hold back the fear.

"He's in the dark. He's lying down. He's in some sort of—I don't know—some sort of box. Container."

Without warning, her breath hitched in her chest.

"Oh, God," she said. "It's a coffin. He's buried in a coffin."

She heard a muffled exclamation. She thought it came from Elmore Granger.

"Okay, take it easy, Amy," Detective Carlson said. "That's an idea the kidnapper could have taken from half a dozen movies. It doesn't mean he's going to leave Nick to die in there. What else can you tell me?"

"It smells funny," Amy said. "Like paint, only stronger."

She took a deep breath. The sharp smell filled her nostrils. She felt her heart begin to race. The impulse to push against the walls of her prison, Nick's prison, was almost overwhelming.

"Not paint. It's something else," she panted. "Something he recognizes. Something that terrifies him."

"What is it? Do you know?" Detective Carlson asked.

Amy shook her head. The smell seemed to fill her entire body. Her heartbeats ratcheted up another notch. Her throat constricted. *I know that smell,* she thought. *What is it?*

As if in answer, everything went still inside her head.

Amy had a sudden vision of herself, but not herself, holding a brush, applying something to a wooden deck. There was a guy next to her doing the exact same thing.

I know who that is, she thought. *That's Pat.*

"I don't know why my dad makes us do this," Pat said. "It almost never rains around here."

Amy's hands clawed at her chest.

"No," she said. "Please, God, no! Don't let it be that."

"That's enough," her father said.

Amy felt the watch being torn from her fingers. The horrible smell, the sense of confinement, vanished. And with it, her knowledge of what the smell meant.

Amy curled up against the back of the couch, forc-

34

ing herself to breathe deeply and slowly.

Breathe the way I'm breathing, Nick, she thought. And wished with all her heart that he could hear her.

She opened her eyes to the overturned coffee table. Across its ruin, five pairs of eyes focused steadily upon her.

Well, she thought, *so much for losing my talent.*

"Oh, fine," she said. "I close my eyes for half a minute and somebody rearranges the furniture."

Detective Carlson gave a strangled laugh. Amy's father ran his hand across his face, then helped her to sit up. Her mother didn't say a word, but moved to sit beside her father. She reached across him to squeeze one of Amy's hands tightly. Amy squeezed back.

Finally, Amy looked at Elmore Granger. He had his head down in his hands. As Amy watched, Steve Dorsey reached down to touch his employer on the shoulder in silent communication. Elmore Granger straightened up at once.

"Yes, thank you, Steve," he said.

His voice was as beautiful as ever. But his dark eyes were turbulent with emotion, and Amy could see his fingers tremble. *We're all shaken,* she thought.

"That was the most remarkable thing I've ever seen, Miss Johnson," Elmore Granger finally said. "I take it," he went on, choosing his words with great care, "that what we just saw you experience is what's actually happening to my son."

It couldn't have been an easy thing for him to say, but his voice hadn't faltered once.

Maybe he can be ruthless after all, Amy thought.

"That's right," she said. "Though what I just experienced was . . . unusually strong."

In fact, she'd never felt anything like it.

Amy had made powerful contact with victims before, but nothing to compare with what she'd felt with

Nick Granger. She'd done more than get inside his mind. See through his eyes. It was as if she'd *become* him.

How else could she explain that sudden memory of working on the deck? A memory she was absolutely sure was not her own.

"I hope what you saw didn't upset you, Mr. Granger," Amy said. "It's one of the reasons I don't often work with family members present."

But you insisted.

Elmore Granger's expression hardened. "Not if the strength of what you experience will help to save my son."

Definitely ruthless, Amy thought.

"Is there something your son is afraid of?" she asked. "I mean *really* afraid, like a phobia, almost?"

"I don't know!" Elmore Granger finally exploded. "My son might as well be a total stranger for all that I know about him. To think if I just knew the right answer to the right question, I might help free him . . ."

His voice trailed off. Steve Dorsey shifted position, as if about to intervene.

"What about from when he lived with you?" Amy swiftly prompted. "When he was small. Whatever he's afraid of, it feels like an old fear. Something that happened before he was old enough to be able to explain it away. It's very powerful."

The elder Granger considered for a moment. Amy became aware of how tired she was. And of Steve Dorsey's considering green eyes studying her face.

"There was a boating accident," Elmore Granger answered slowly. "The summer Nick's mother and I were divorced. A squall came up, the boom swept over. Nick got knocked overboard. He couldn't swim. He still can't, as a matter of fact. He hates to go near the water. After the accident, he wouldn't even take a bath.''

Amy felt something like a giant fist form in the pit of her stomach.

"Water," she whispered.

"What is it?" her father said.

The fist gave one vicious punch. And Amy knew the answer.

"The smell," she said. "I recognize it."

She closed her eyes and began to rock back and forth on the couch. The images she'd seen, the things she'd experienced, played back just inside her eyelids. An endless loop of fear and pain.

Only this time she understood them. She knew exactly what they meant.

"Nick is in a coffin," she said. "But that isn't why he's so frightened. That isn't what terrifies him. What terrifies him is the smell. Because he recognizes it. Because he's afraid it can only mean one thing."

"What?" her father asked, his voice sharp. "What does he smell? What does it mean? You're not making sense yet, Amy."

"It's varnish," Amy said. "*Waterproof* varnish."

"Waterproof," Detective Carlson echoed. "Merciful God in heaven."

Amy opened her eyes and forced herself to look into the expression in Elmore Granger's. She thought it was the bleakest sight she'd ever seen.

"Nick's coffin isn't underground. It's *underwater*, Mr. Granger," she whispered. "Nick is terrified his kidnapper is going to drown him."

seven
♂

Somebody had been inside his head.

Either that, or he had gone insane.

At least it was easier to breathe now. And he thought the mystery guest had done it. So he supposed he should be grateful.

He lay in his box, the box he was trying so hard not to think of as his coffin. His back and legs ached from being forced to lie in one position for so long. His hands were raw and scraped from the way he'd beat them in desperation against the top of his prison.

Don't think about it, he told himself. *There's nothing you can do about it. Just stay calm. Just keep breathing.*

In. Out. In. Out. Deep and slow. Calm and steady. The way the voice inside his head had told him.

Breathe the way I'm breathing, Nick, she had said. Just before she vanished. He didn't know which upset him more. That she had been there in the first place or that she had left him.

But it was doing as the voice suggested that gave him the miracle. The one he hadn't even known to hope for.

Body finally relaxed, heartbeat finally steady, Nicholas Granger slipped into a sleep that had no dreams.

* * *

When he awoke, he didn't know how much later, the first thing he knew was that he wasn't alone. He could feel the other presence filling his head like a powerful fragrance.

This time he didn't fight it. He lay still and let it come.

Bright pictures flashed before his eyes that could see only darkness. A baseball diamond in the early morning, its sprinklers sending water in high arcs over the green grass. The pages of a book, turning in a glow of yellow lamplight. A full white moon hanging in a sky of spangling stars.

Simple things. Ordinary things. Things he hadn't even known he loved. Until they'd been so abruptly and horribly taken away from him.

Is this better? the voice said. *Does this help? Can you even see the images I'm sending?*

Yes, he thought. *Oh, yes, yes, yes.*

The outside world is here, Nick. We haven't forgotten you.

But even as he heard the thought, the images were fading, the darkness creeping back across his vision.

He reached for them, his hands clunking against the top of his box. He could feel the panic flooding back, cold and potent. Lethal.

"No," he said aloud. Why not? There wasn't anybody there to hear him. "No, don't go."

I have to, the voice said. *I can't do this for very long. But I'll look for a way to make the link stronger, Nick. So I can find out where you are.*

It faded. Stopped.

"No!" Nick shouted, desperate now. "Don't leave me here. Don't let me die alone."

He knew the second the other mind returned, curling around his in what he swore was an embrace. He

39

clung to it, wanting to stay wrapped up there forever.
Don't worry, Nick. I won't.

"I won't, Nick," Amy promised. "I won't. I won't."

Completely exhausted, she leaned her head against her bedroom window, tears running unheeded down her cheeks, and let Nick Granger's watch drop from her numb fingers to the floor.

eight
ℒ

"*Do you have any idea how much water there is in* the state of Washington?" asked Carl.

It was after dinner. Amy, her father, and the detective were ranged around the dining room table with a map of Washington spread out before them.

Amy had to admit, it was a pretty daunting sight. The map had an awful lot of blue on it, most of it in the western part of the state.

She heard her mother running water in the kitchen as she did the dinner dishes. *Water, water, everywhere,* Amy thought. And remembered, belatedly, that it was her turn to do the washing up.

"Show me where Nick and his father live again," she said, pushing aside her one remaining piece of silverware. Wishing it was as easy to push away her exhaustion.

She'd never been so tired in her life. But then, she'd never had such a strong connection with anyone before. Not even with Brian Newcomb.

Surely, the strength of her connection with Nick was a positive sign, Amy thought. Maybe it meant she wasn't destined to fail, but was instead destined to succeed and find him.

"Here," her father answered, leaning over to point at the map.

Not surprisingly, the Grangers lived in an exclusive neighborhood. A gated community on what locals called "the East Side."

That meant the east side of Lake Washington, Amy remembered. Across the lake from Seattle. She stared at her father's finger.

"Then they're right on the shores of Lake Washington."

Carl nodded his agreement. "That's correct."

"Right on the water," Amy persisted.

Once more, Carl nodded. "That's correct," he said again. "I see where you're going, Amy. I've already taken care of it. There's a team of divers in the water even as we speak."

Amy concentrated on not squirming in her chair as Carl continued with his explanation. Worrying about Nick Granger was making her itchy.

She could still feel his fear crawling just beneath the surface of her skin. Her whole body ached with the effort she was making not to scratch it. Amy was sure her fingers would come away bloody.

"I called the request for divers in just after Granger and his fashion-model-for-an-assistant departed," Carl went on. He slid a sideways glance at Amy.

"Just about the time your mom had hustled you off to your room, if I remember right."

"I made tea. Would anyone like some?" said a voice from the kitchen doorway.

Amy turned to find her mother standing between the dining room and kitchen, cradling a steaming pot in her hands.

"It's Darjeeling, Amy's favorite. But I can make herbal, too, if you'd prefer that, Detective."

"Herbal," Carl said. "You mean like made from weeds or something?"

Amy's mother's lips actually twitched. Amy felt a rush of an emotion she couldn't quite identify.

First, dinner. Barbecued salmon, also Amy's favorite. As if her mother had wanted to prepare the thing she knew Amy enjoyed the most so she'd want to eat to keep up her strength.

Now the kind of tea she liked best, even though Amy didn't usually do caffeine at night. For someone who objected so strongly to what her daughter was doing, Rebecca Johnson was making quite an effort.

"Want some help with the cups, Mom?" Amy asked.

Her mother's eyes rested on her briefly, something Amy couldn't quite recognize glimmering in their depths.

I'm not making it up, Amy thought. *Something really is happening.*

Ever since the moment, earlier in the day, when her mother had reached for her hand, Amy'd had the sense that something was different. That her mother was trying to understand the choice Amy had made. That she was trying to make the effort to support her. Her mother had always stayed aloof from Amy's dealings with the police.

Again, Amy felt the sudden rush of emotion. Only this time she recognized it.

It was hope. Hope that her family would finally work together. That they would finally be a team.

It was what Nick's dad had wanted, too, Amy remembered suddenly. And shivered as she felt the itch move beneath her skin. At least her family was off to a better start, she thought as she looked at her mom again.

Much as it had embarrassed Amy to be whisked off to her room like a two-year-old, she had to admit her mother's quick action had given her a break she'd desperately needed.

The chance to get away from all those eyes, staring at her, silently asking all those questions she still couldn't answer. Any kind of contact wore her out for hours, even days sometimes, but this one had left her particularly exhausted.

Even so, the moment she was alone Amy hadn't hesitated to do the thing her instincts demanded. To try to contact Nick again. As if she could sense his desperate need for reassurance—and her own need to provide it.

She still didn't know quite what to make of the strength of their connection. The intimate way they could communicate. She only knew she was totally committed to doing whatever it took to find him.

"No, thank you, Amy," her mother said, answering her question. "I'm already up. I'll get them."

She set the teapot on the table, went back to the kitchen, and returned with a tray with cups and saucers, milk, and sugar. She set it down beside the teapot.

"I'm going to make a couple of phone calls from my office," she said, pausing to rest her hands briefly on her husband's shoulders. "I think I've finally got a good lead on a space for the new gallery."

"That's great, Mom," Amy said. She knew it had been hard for her mom not to be able to do her own work once the family had moved to Washington.

"Get a good price," Amy's dad said, his fingers reaching up to tangle with his wife's.

"Oh, yeah, that's me," Rebecca Johnson said. "Ms. Killer Negotiator."

"They'd be crazy not to want you," Amy said supportively.

A look of slow pleasure spread across her mother's face. "Why, thank you, Amy. Don't stay up too late, now," she went on, once again all business.

"You know you need a lot of sleep when you"— her voice stumbled just a little—"do this work. See to it, Stan," Rebecca Johnson said, giving her husband's shoulder a firm squeeze before she moved off. "Good night, Detective Carlson."

"Good night, Mrs. Johnson," Carl said.

At the last possible moment, Amy's mother paused at the entrance to the hallway. She turned back. Her eyes rested on the group assembled around the table.

This time Amy knew what she saw in her mother's eyes. Both fear and regret were there. But there was resolution, too. And her mother's voice was steady as she answered.

"As you're on a first-name basis with everyone else in the house, you might as well be with me, too," she said. "My name is Rebecca, Detective."

"Carl," Detective Carlson said.

"Carl," Amy's mother echoed with a nod of her head. "I'm trusting you to take care of my daughter, Carl." Then she turned and vanished down the darkened hallway.

Amy and her father shared a startled glance. But for the first time that day, the first time in almost as long as she could remember, Amy's heart lightened.

Maybe she no longer needed to defend her decisions to her mother. Maybe now her mother would come to her defense.

She rose to pour Carl the first cup of tea.

"Tell me why you don't think Nick Granger is in the water just off his father's own property."

"It's too obvious," Carl said.

At some point Amy no longer remembered, the team had switched locations back to the living room. Carl now cradled his third cup of tea in his hands. They'd been going over the same point, over and over.

"It's only obvious if you know he's underwater,"

Amy answered. "That's a leap most people aren't going to make."

"That's true," Carl admitted.

"But you still don't expect the dive team to find anything," Amy persisted.

Carl set his cup down on a coaster on the coffee table. "No, I don't," he said. "There's something about this whole thing that just feels funny."

"What have you got?" Amy deadpanned. "Second sight?"

Carl looked startled for just a second. Then he let out a quick bark of laughter.

They were a good team, Amy thought. And they were going to solve this. They were going to find Nick Granger.

"You don't think the kidnapper is after Granger's money, do you?" Stan Johnson spoke up.

Carl switched his attention to Amy's father.

"No, I don't," he said again. "I think it's about Granger himself. About trying to get him out in the open."

"But why?" Amy asked.

Carl picked the cup back up again, as if he thought better when he was holding it. "Granger made his money designing defense systems," he said. "And offensive ones."

"Weapons of mass destruction," Amy murmured.

"Exactly," Carl said.

"So you think this is some sort of even-the-scales domestic terrorism? Weapons of mass destruction don't kill people, people do?"

"Hey." Carl held up one hand. "I didn't say it had to make sense to us, only to the guy who's doing it."

"Actually," Amy's dad put in, "it's not a bad scenario. It would explain why the kidnapper's given us such a long time line to find Nick Granger. Long enough for his father to come out to play."

"And that's why I don't think Nick is in the water off his father's estate," Carl finished. "If whoever's doing this can get that close, he can get to Elmore Granger. There'd be no need to take the son at all."

"Assuming this is really about the father in the first place," Amy said. Abruptly, she shivered. *How long?* she thought. *How long before Nick can't stand it any longer?*

"Yes," Carl acknowledged. "Assuming that."

"So what happens next?" Amy asked.

The phone rang.

"Somebody answers the phone," Carl said. "With luck, that's the report from the dive team."

Stan Johnson sprinted for the telephone, picking up on the third ring. Amy rubbed her arms again as she and Carl sat in the living room listening to Amy's father's voice.

"What?" Carl said.

"I'm itchy," Amy explained. "It's like Nick is still there, right under my skin. I've never felt anything like this. It's like there's a circuit open between Nick and me all the time, but I can only tap into it for short periods."

She paused, hoping Carl wouldn't think she was starting to lose her grip already.

"There isn't anything to suggest that Nick Granger might be—like me—is there?" she asked.

Carl's surprise was evident on his face. "You mean a clairvoyant?"

Amy nodded. "I was just thinking that could explain the weird connection."

"I don't think so," Carl answered. He opened his notebook and flipped through it rapidly. "About the only thing that might add up is that he's never mingled much. Always been a loner. But there are lots of things that could account for that."

"That's true," Amy said. "Like being the son of

one of the wealthiest men on the planet. It's just—I don't want us to lose sight of what's happening to Nick, even if we do decide this is really all about his father.

"Nick's the one who's frightened, Carl. He's the one who's been taken. We can't afford to forget that."

Can't afford to lose him.

Carl reached over to touch Amy's agitated hands briefly. "Don't worry. We won't, Amy."

As she heard the echo of her own words to Nick in Detective Carlson's voice, Amy shivered once again.

Her father came back into the living room.

"You were right. That was the dive team."

"And?" Carl asked.

"Nothing," Stan Johnson answered. "You were right about that, too. The protection on Elmore Granger has been increased, but it's perimeter only. He wouldn't agree to anyone inside the house."

"Figures," Carl said.

"I want to go there," Amy said suddenly. "To the house. I want to spend some time in Nick's room. Maybe I can find something else important to him. Something that will help me sustain the contact longer so we can find out where he is."

"You're sure about this?" her father said. "This connection is already way off the charts, Amy."

"I'm sure, Dad," Amy said.

"Okay," her father answered, drawing the syllables out slowly, his blue eyes on her pale face. "I'll want to tag along, though."

Amy rolled her eyes. "Oh, man," she said. "Not you again."

"Tough noogies," her father said.

Amy grinned. Carl's head moved back and forth, as if he were watching a tennis match.

"Don't you guys ever give it a rest?" he asked.

Amy shrugged. "Releases tension."

"Personally, I prefer a cold beer," Carl said.

Amy's grin got a little bigger. "I'm underage, Detective."

"Right," Carl said. He got to his feet. "I'll see if I can arrange a visit on my way home tonight. I'll let you know the time first thing in the morning. In the meantime, I suggest we all get a good night's sleep. There's nothing else we can do at the moment."

Except pray, Amy thought. But she didn't say it.

Instead, she followed her dad to the door as he let Detective Carlson out. Then she stood at the front window, watching as his red taillights disappeared around the corner.

"You okay, sport?" her father asked.

"Okay," Amy answered. "I think I'll take Carl's advice and go to bed now, Dad."

"See you in the morning," her father answered. He leaned down to kiss the top of Amy's head. "Sweet dreams, Amy."

I will if I can, Dad.

"You, too."

Back in her room, Amy pulled her nightshirt on, then climbed into bed. She put her arms around Funny One and pulled the old clown close. Then she reached down and tucked Nick Granger's watch under her mattress.

She wanted to have it close, but not somewhere where she could reach out and touch it accidentally.

Just call me the princess and the pea, she thought.

And wished with all her heart that, like all good fairy tales, this story would have a happy ending.

nine
𝒟

𝒮he awoke to pitch darkness. Mouth dry. Heart pounding. Her body locked in place.

My legs, she thought. *Why can't I move my legs? Oh, God. Where am I?*

She twisted her head back and forth in desperation. And felt her heartbeats ease when she realized she could see the numbers on her digital clock.

The glowing numbers said it was 3:00 A.M. Sliding toward, but not yet, morning. If she lay just like this long enough, face toward the window, she would see the sun come up.

She was in her own room. In her own bed. With trembling hands, Amy reached down to touch her legs. And discovered her own sheets wrapped tightly around them.

Dreaming, she thought. *I've been dreaming.*

Of a place without light or movement. A place wrapped around her so tightly she'd wrapped herself in her own shroud as she'd dreamed of it.

Dreaming of Nick Granger's coffin.

Amy clawed the sheets from her legs and got out of bed. She staggered across the room to take up her usual position on the window seat. It didn't matter that she couldn't see the view. The window seat was still where she felt safest.

She rubbed her legs, forcing the circulation back into them, then winced when they began to tingle and sting. But the pain was better than nothing, she thought. And tried not to think about whether or not Nick Granger was in pain.

If she started to play "what if" she would drown in her own fears. Then she would never find him, no matter how strong their connection.

Amy returned to the bed, picked up Funny One, and carried him to the window seat. Then she reached behind the back window seat cushion and brought out her sketchbook.

She crossed to her desk to light a candle and took a fresh stick of charcoal from a holder on top of the desk. Finally, she moved back to the window seat, flipped open the sketchbook, and set the softly glowing candle on the windowsill.

In the long months since the fire of the Rising Dawn, the death of Brian Newcomb, the months of nightmares that seemed never-ending, this had been Amy's only comfort. The only thing that kept the horror at bay.

She never turned on her bedroom light. Never wanted her parents to know that she was up and worry.

Instead, the rough charcoal firmly between her fingers, Amy sketched the images of her dreams in the hope that, if she could only draw them all and face them, then the nightmares would go away.

In a way, she supposed it had worked. Because, gradually, Amy had stopped filling page after page with pictures of death and destruction, and started filling them with a young man's face.

The face of the guy she'd met just once, on the day of the fire. The guy with whom she'd had no more than a casual conversation. But it had seemed so easy, so right, that a door had opened in Amy's heart. To a chamber she hadn't even known was there.

What would it be like to have someone like him with her always? Someone she could trust and confide in, a soul mate.

But she'd had no time to discover whether or not he was what she so hoped, because her whole world had burst into flame.

By the time it subsided, Brian Newcomb, the forty-two members of the Rising Dawn cult, and their charismatic leader were dead. Their bodies nearly unidentifiable, burned to ashes by the heat of the fire.

And Amy's chance for love was over before it even began. Before she even learned his name.

She knew now that sketching him would never help her find him. But still, the ritual was soothing. Familiar in a world that had once again grown strange.

Amy tucked her legs up underneath her, flipped to a fresh page in her sketchbook, touched the tip of the charcoal to the clean white paper, and began to draw a face.

Large, almond-shaped eyes. Amy bore down on the charcoal to give them darkness, luster. Stubborn chin. Broad forehead. The kind of face you didn't give up on, she thought. The kind that didn't give up on you.

Her own eyes half closed, she continued working, sharpening lines, adding details. The soft scratch of charcoal against thick paper the only sound. The glow from the single candle the only illumination.

Till she opened her eyes and held the sketchbook up in front of her, examining her handiwork.

And felt her heart squeeze in her chest.

No, Amy thought. *I didn't mean it. I didn't* do *that.* But she had.

She slapped her hand down on top of the candle, extinguishing it, hardly noticing the pain as the flame licked against the palm of her hand.

Then she reached for Funny One, holding him close

even as she pressed the sketchbook to her chest. She rocked the old clown back and forth. Back and forth. Not caring that the charcoal stained the front of her nightshirt. Only caring about one thing.

She wasn't crazy. Wasn't going to go crazy. She could control her own fears. Her own destiny. She knew the difference between the present and the past, and didn't have to let the past control her.

Telling herself over and over that what happened then didn't mean she was going to fail Nick Granger.

But still she rocked, until the glow of the red numbers on her clock's face faded as the dawn began to stain the sky. Until the drawing she'd made was smudged almost beyond recognition and she could see it clearly only in her mind's eye.

She'd drawn his face inside a coffin, just like Nick Granger's.

ten

*"**N**aturally, Mr. Granger is more than happy to assist* in the investigation by making the compound available to you and your father, Miss Johnson," said Steve Dorsey the next morning as he met them on the brick steps of the Granger house.

Amy wasn't quite sure the word *house* did the structure justice. *Mansion* might be a better choice. She'd never seen a house so big, except on reruns of *Lifestyles of the Rich and Famous.*

And then there'd been the security checkpoints.

The guard at the gate to the whole community had been first. Then there'd been the guards at the electric gates to the Granger estate itself. Guards who came complete with guns and thickly muscled, big-toothed dogs.

Granger's regular guards had been supplemented by uniformed police officers. From Carl, Amy knew there were others patrolling the perimeter of the grounds.

Once through the front gate, Amy and her father had driven down a long drive with tall hedges bordering both sides. The same kind of hedge that bordered the front of the property, flanking the front gate.

Amy didn't know what kind of plant the hedge was made of, but she could see that it had long, sharp

54

thorns. It was plain you could only get into Elmore Granger's "compound" if he wanted you to.

"But I'm sure you'll understand—" Amy yanked her attention back to the present as Steve Dorsey opened one of two massive front doors and stepped inside. Amy saw a flagstone entryway stretching out endlessly before her.

"I'm sure you'll understand that a man like Mr. Granger is far too busy to conduct your tour himself."

Amy made eye contact with her father. Stan Johnson closed one eye. *Well, at least I'm not making all this up,* Amy thought. Her father saw the same things she did. Steve Dorsey was definitely into making sure they knew his employer was important. And so was he.

Aloud she simply said, "Of course."

Amy's body ached; her eyes were scratchy. Her head felt full, the way it did right before she caught a cold. But she knew she wasn't getting sick. She was worried about Nick Granger. She was worried about herself.

And she wasn't the only one, she thought, as her father stepped into the entry hall and closed the door behind them. Amy knew her father was concerned about her. Knew he'd spotted her pale skin and blood-shot eyes.

But after one quick glance at Amy's tired face at the breakfast table that morning, her father hadn't asked any questions. He hadn't probed.

For that, Amy was grateful. She wasn't sure she was ready to talk about what was going on. Wasn't sure she understood it herself.

It was as if her connection with Nick Granger was so unique, so powerful, it was pulling her whole life toward it. Everything was getting mixed up. Running together like sidewalk chalk in the rain. With Nick

Granger slowly but surely becoming the focal point. The only constant.

"All right," Steve Dorsey said, interrupting Amy's troubled reverie. "Let's get going."

An hour later, Amy's head was swimming, and all she wanted to do was sit down.

Steve Dorsey had taken them through the house at a brisk pace, and it had still taken a solid hour. Even then, they hadn't seen the whole thing.

Naturally, Dorsey had explained in his tight, self-important voice, Amy and her father couldn't expect to be admitted into Elmore Granger's private quarters.

Of course not, Amy's father had answered. They'd never anticipated such an honor. And they'd never dream of interrupting Mr. Granger at his work.

That reply had pleased Steve Dorsey so much he'd unbent enough to answer Stan Johnson's questions about the state-of-the-art electronics the house boasted.

Motion detectors. Temperature control. Lights that went on when you entered a room, that grew brighter or dimmed as you raised or lowered your voice.

Amy half suspected there were security cameras hidden behind the eyes of pictures, though her other half admitted she was being fanciful. Still, she couldn't shake the sense that she was being watched everywhere she went.

Perhaps it was the incredible quiet. With the exception of the flagstone entry, the rest of the rooms were carpeted. Thick-piled carpet that muffled any noise.

Even the polished wood hallways had runners on them. Amy noticed that Steve Dorsey had been careful to walk in the very center of each one. His feet never coming anywhere near the hardwood floors.

There hadn't been so much as a speck of dust or a sofa cushion out of place in the entire house. The place Elmore Granger had chosen as a home for his son was a showplace. Expensive furnishings, impeccably maintained.

And it was about as homey as a chrome-and-Formica laboratory, Amy thought. She remembered her unmade bed with satisfaction.

"Perhaps you'd care to see the grounds now," Steve Dorsey said. "That's the area of the compound where Mr. Granger is making the most changes."

Amy almost protested. She wanted to see where Nick lived, of course. But more important was the time she might spend in his room. That was the real purpose of the trip.

But, out of the corner of her eye, she caught the slight narrowing of her father's eyes, the shake of his head. During their years of working together, Amy and her father had become adept at reading one another's silent signals.

Now she recognized that her father didn't want her to press the issue of Nick's room yet.

"What kind of changes?" Amy asked.

Steve Dorsey moved rapidly down the huge central staircase, exactly in the center of the runner once again.

"He's adding a series of sports facilities," he answered as he reached the bottom of the staircase and strode across the entry hall flagstones.

The heels of his shoes made sharp clicking sounds. Almost as if the entry hall was part of the security system, Amy thought. You could hear anybody coming or going.

For the first time, she wondered if Carl might be right after all. Maybe Nick's kidnapping was about getting to his father. Getting Elmore Granger to come out in the open.

"We won't be able to enter all of them, since some are still under construction," Dorsey went on. He held the door open as Amy and her father preceded him onto the steps.

"But you should definitely see them to fully comprehend the effort Mr. Granger is making on Nick's behalf."

The effort he's making, Amy thought. Once again, she wondered if Steve Dorsey's carefully chosen words reflected his own viewpoint or his employer's.

How did Steve Dorsey feel about Nick Granger? Amy wondered. Before Nick's arrival, had Dorsey hoped he was the heir apparent? Had Nick's presence ruined some cherished plan?

"We'd like to see them very much," said Amy's father as he and Amy followed Steve Dorsey away from the house down a well-maintained path. Like the drive, the path was bordered by thick, high hedges, making any sort of overview of the property impossible.

The path was made of nutshells, Amy noticed as she walked along. Hazelnuts, she thought. They crunched underfoot, a friendly sort of sound. The first she'd heard since entering the Granger compound.

Amy bore down a little harder. The shells gave a satisfying crack. Then, abruptly, she realized the path could serve the same purpose as the flagstone entry. Its sound identified the location of anyone walking on it.

"What kind of additions is Mr. Granger making?" she asked.

"There were outdoor tennis courts already on the property," Steve Dorsey answered. He paused at a break in the hedge. Through it, Amy could see two tennis courts, one surfaced with vivid red clay. The other with bright green grass.

A high fence surrounded each court. Mounted on

the top of each support pole, Amy could see an array of cameras. Some pointed toward the court, some toward the surrounding grounds. As Steve Dorsey stepped through the opening in the hedge, the closest cameras swiveled toward him.

"Mr. Granger has added an indoor hard court," Dorsey said, a wave of his hand indicating the new construction.

The building was made of wood, designed to fit into the landscape. The top was fitted with skylights so that, even when indoors, players could feel they were out in the open. The indoor court, too, was ringed with motion sensors.

"Impressive," Amy's dad commented.

"Mr. Granger also has plans for an indoor track," Dorsey went on. "The fully equipped exercise gymnasium is already complete. You can see it through the trees just there." He pointed. "And then there is the Olympic-sized lap pool, but that is still under construction."

"He's building his son a pool even though he knows Nick can't swim?" Amy blurted out before she could help it. She could practically see Steve Dorsey bristle.

"Mr. Granger felt it would be appropriate for Nick to confront his fears," he replied in a stiff voice.

Amy felt a spurt of intense dislike. It was probably perfectly natural for Elmore Granger to want Nick to overcome his fear of the water. Perhaps it was even what Nick himself wanted. But Steve Dorsey made it sound like the "appropriate" way for Nick to confront his fears would be for his father to toss him in and time how long he stayed there.

"Naturally, construction on the lap pool has been halted. Mr. Granger felt it would be . . . insensitive of him to continue in the present circumstances."

Very touching, Amy thought sarcastically.

"Do you suppose I could tour the inside of the gym?" Amy's father broke the silence. "I love a good workout."

"Of course," Dorsey answered automatically. "If you'll just come this way." He turned toward the path that led around the indoor tennis court to the gym.

"While Steve and I are doing that, you can have that time you wanted in Nick's room, Amy," her father finished smoothly.

Steve Dorsey skidded to a halt, the nutshells snapping underneath his heels as he swung around.

Way to go, Dad, Amy thought.

Now she knew why he'd wanted her to accompany him on the tour of the sports facilities. He'd wanted to create the opportunity to split the party up, give her the chance to spend time in Nick's room alone, without the hovering presence of Steve Dorsey.

"Oh, but . . ." Steve Dorsey faltered. It was the first time Amy'd seen him at a loss. She pressed her advantage quickly, not wanting to give him time to recover.

"Naturally," she said, doing her best to match the tone Steve used at his most officious, "we cleared this request with Mr. Granger. I believe Detective Carlson handled the matter himself. I'm sure you'll want to see your employer's wishes carried out."

The angle of Steve Dorsey's jaw grew even sharper. "Certainly, Miss Johnson," he finally ground out. "I'll just take you back to the house."

"That really isn't necessary, is it?" Amy asked sweetly. "I'll just follow this path. You two can return in a little while. Enjoy your tour, Dad. Don't pump too much iron."

Before Steve Dorsey had a chance to offer further resistance, Amy stepped around him and headed back toward the house. The whole time, she could feel Dorsey's sharp green eyes boring into her back. It made her shoulder blades itch.

What is going on around here? she thought.

eleven
D

He should have known he couldn't trust it. The voice, the presence that had been his only comfort. His only hope.

Like everything else in his life, every*one* else, it had made him promises it couldn't keep and then abandoned him. Left him all alone.

He'd loved and trusted his mother, and she had died and left him. He didn't yet know his father well enough to know if he was someone it was safe to trust. He knew he didn't trust Steve Dorsey. Everything about him screamed "Shark!"

And so he was alone. The way he'd always been. Though nothing in his life could possibly have prepared him for the way he was alone now.

At least the darkness didn't bother him anymore.

Actually, he'd gotten so he almost liked it. The dark was like another person, a companion trapped with him inside his box. It flowed around him, snuggled up against him. It was there when he fell asleep, every time he opened his eyes.

There was no sense of time inside his prison. No way to mark the passage of it in the world outside.

The glow of his watch face might have informed him, he knew, but the hands that had taken his freedom had taken that also. The sting of the metal band being dragged across his wrist was the last thing he remembered before the sickly sweet smell that had sent him plunging headfirst into oblivion.

He couldn't feel the lower part of his body any longer. His legs had ached, then cramped, then gone completely numb. But his arms still worked, dragging the bag of drinking water he'd thought was a hallucination at first up toward his face to take sip after tiny sip.

It was the only time water had ever given him hope.

Why give him water to drink if they were going to leave him here to die? That didn't make sense, did it?

Sense.

He opened his mouth to the darkness and laughed aloud.

The moment he could make sense of this would be the moment he'd know he'd truly lost it.

Before he could stop it, the laugh had turned into a sob.

I don't want to be here. I don't want to die alone. In the dark.

Where are you? he thought, as if his question could will the other presence into existence. *Why don't you come back to me?*

Why did you have to go?

twelve

Amy stood in the center of Nick's bedroom, turning a slow circle as she studied the plain, white walls.

The room was like the box of possessions Nick's father had brought her, she thought. Like the rest of the house. Virtually a clean slate. On the surface, at least, there was nothing there to tell her who Nick Granger really was.

I don't even know what he looks like, Amy realized.

Amy'd seen no family portraits, no pictures of Nick and his father, during her tour of the house. She supposed that made sense, since Nick had grown up with his mother. But still—

Operating totally on instinct, Amy walked swiftly across the room and yanked open Nick's top desk drawer. Pens. Pencils. Paper clips. Exactly what anyone might expect to find, and no more.

Amy pushed the drawer shut and opened the second drawer. Paper, neatly stacked. Stamps. Envelopes. The third drawer was virtually empty, as if Nick didn't use it at all.

Feeling frustrated, Amy knelt and yanked the bottom drawer so hard she pulled it clear out of the desk. Startled, she toppled over backward and sat down, hard, on the floor.

Great. This one must be empty, too, she thought.

But her years spent working cases had taught her to be thorough. She settled the deep drawer in her lap and peered inside. And felt her heart kick as she realized what she'd discovered.

In the very bottom lay a gold picture frame, face-down.

Praying that she hadn't found some picture of baby Nick naked on a white bearskin rug, Amy reached down and turned the frame over. The picture within it was hard to see in the depths of the drawer. Amy lifted it out into the sunlight and felt her whole body tingle in shock.

"Oh, my God."

Two guys stared out of the frame at her, one dark, one blond. The blond one's blue eyes twinkled with mischief at the camera. One elbow leaned casually on the shoulder of the dark-haired guy at his side.

With one hand, the blond pointed at the burgundy sweater the dark-haired guy was wearing. With the other, he made rabbit ears behind his head. The dark-haired guy squinted a little at the camera, his mouth pursed as if trying not to laugh, as if he knew exactly what was going on.

"Yo, Nick," read an inscription across the bottom. "Mom says she's glad you like the sweater, but those ears have got to go. I'm coming to see you in Seattle. Count on it. Pat."

Amy closed her eyes. In the silence of her mind, she conjured up an image, the face she'd been drawing for months now. The face she'd drawn just the night before, trapped inside a coffin. When she opened her eyes, the dark eyes of the guy in the photo looked back.

Nick Granger was the guy she'd met so briefly, yet fallen so hard for. The guy from San Francisco.

No wonder, Amy thought as she felt her heart begin to beat in heavy strokes. *No wonder our connection was so strong.* She'd already been dreaming of him, day and night.

Galvanized, Amy leaped to her feet and began to move about the room, still gripping the photograph tightly in one hand.

It has to be here somewhere, she thought.

Somewhere in Nick's room was the reason she'd wanted to come here in the first place: the object that would provide the strongest possible link because it was a thing that mattered to him. Something from the past, not tainted by his current fear.

But what was it. And where?

Abruptly, Amy realized she was clutching the picture frame so hard its sharp edges were digging into her hand. She forced herself to relax her grip and look at the picture again.

The answer was right there.

The burgundy sweater, Amy thought. The one Pat's mom had made for him.

Amy sprinted for Nick's dresser. She didn't waste time with the top drawers, but fell to her knees before the one on the bottom. The bottom drawer of her dresser was where Amy'd kept Funny One when she'd wanted him safe and out of sight.

Please, let me be right about this, she thought. *Let Nick have done what I would have done.*

She took a deep breath, set the picture on the floor beside her, and pulled open the bottom dresser drawer. Swiftly, Amy rooted through its contents. Winter sweaters, a faint smell of mothballs wafting up around her.

The first two piles were all navy blue. Part of Nick's school uniform, probably. Heart pounding, Amy reached for the final pile of sweaters, sorting through them. Underneath the last one, she found what she'd been looking for.

The sweater was a rich burgundy color. The fisherman's knit cabling was thick, the sweater well-worn. It wasn't scratchy the way some wool sweaters were. It had aged soft.

As Amy pulled it from the drawer, handling it sent a tingle like a mild electric shock running up and down both of her arms.

That was good, but not good enough. Not a strong enough connection to put her back inside Nick Granger's mind. Running on instinct once again, Amy lifted the sweater and thrust her head and arms inside.

It was like falling into deep water. A sudden shock followed by slow motion. Amy could almost see herself sinking through different levels of consciousness. A tiny part of her that was just Amy, all Amy, floated up above.

But the rest of her plunged deeper, deeper, toward the swift current waiting at the very bottom. The current that was Nick Granger's thoughts. She had a moment of wild disorientation as it caught her and pulled her along.

And then, suddenly, all was still, the contact complete. Being with Nick was like being in the heart of a storm. Rough waters roared all around her, but Amy sat within a circle of complete calm.

Nick Granger's voice, his thoughts, were clear as a bell. As if he and Amy were one. Not "two minds with but a single thought" any longer. Not ever again. But two thoughts with but a single mind.

She'd never felt a contact quite like this. Never even dreamed it could be possible. Her fingers trembled as she pulled the sweater all the way over her head.

There you are, she heard Nick say. *Oh, God. Oh, God. I thought you'd left for good. That you were never coming back. I thought you'd lied to me.*

It's all right, Nick, Amy thought. *I'm here now. Calm down. I can't stay in touch this way all the time.*

I'm not strong enough. And I'm still figuring out how this works.

She could have sworn she heard a scrap of desperate laughter. *How WHAT works?* Nick Granger thought. *You mean you understand this? You know what's going on?*

Amy felt a sudden fear move through her body like a gust of winter wind before she could respond.

Not her feelings. Not her fear. Nick Granger's.

I'm going crazy, aren't I? She heard his desperate thought. *That's what's going on, isn't it? Either that or you're one of them. You're in this somehow. You want to hurt me. You want me to die.*

No, Nick, that's not true, Amy sent back swiftly, strongly. *I'm on your side. I want to get you out of there.*

Out of WHERE?

Amy took a deep breath. It was the million-dollar question. Actually, it was the ten-million-dollar one. That's how much the kidnapper wanted to free Nick Granger—if she couldn't free him first.

That's what I want you to help me find out.

thirteen

I don't know how I can do that, *Nick thought*. I *don't understand what you want.*

Amy could feel his panic, his disorientation, lurking just below the surface of his thoughts.

Nick wanted the contact with her, longed for it even, but it also frightened him. He didn't understand what it was.

Amy closed her eyes and reached out. Trying to fill Nick with her hope. To wrap him in it, the way she wished that she could wrap him in her arms.

She could feel him reaching back. His need entwining tightly with her own. Until she could no longer distinguish one from the other. And in that moment a longing swept through Amy, a longing stronger than anything she'd ever known.

The desire to believe that, this time, things would be different. This time, it was safe to let the barriers down. To trust. To love.

Who are you? she heard him whisper. *How is this possible?*

I think . . . Amy began, then faltered. She pulled in a deep breath, then took the plunge. *I think it's because we've met before.*

Before, Nick echoed. *Oh, you mean the last time.*

No, Amy answered. *I—*

What's your name? Nick interrupted. *Tell me who you are.*

My name is Amy. Amy Johnson.

Amy, he said, his voice a caress. *I can trust you, can't I?*

You can trust me, Nick, Amy answered, abandoning her attempt to get him to remember. Now was not the time. There would be time later, after she'd rescued him. Plenty of time. Right now she had to get him out of danger.

If I ask you a question, will you tell me the truth? Nick asked. *Even if you think the answer isn't what I want?*

I'll tell you the truth, Nick. I swear it.

There was a slight pause, as if he were gathering the courage to face what must come next.

I'm going to die in this place, aren't I?

Amy's reaction was swift and visceral. Her whole body shook with the force of her denial.

No! she thought back vehemently. She could not let that happen. Would not. Particularly not now that she knew who he was.

I'm going to get you out of there, Nick. I promise.

She could feel the despair running through him like quicksilver. Feel how hard he tried to battle it back.

I trust you, he said. *God knows I want to believe you. I just don't understand how. How can what we're doing, what we have, save me?*

Your mind may be storing images, Amy answered. *Important details you don't consciously know. If I can pick up on those images, I might be able to recognize them, find out where you are. Think back on what happened the day you were kidnapped, Nick. Tell me anything you can remember.*

A kaleidoscope of images flooded Amy as Nick concentrated. But they were too fragmented, too jumbled all together for her to make any sense of them.

Part of her wanted to beg him to slow down, but another part was terrified to stop the flow of his recollections.

Somewhere in his memory, Amy was sure, was the key, the image that would free him.

I can't remember very much, he finally answered. *I'd gone into downtown Seattle to run an errand for my father. Dorsey was supposed to do it, but at the last minute he handed it off.*

Wait a minute, Amy sent, trying to control the adrenaline spiking through her. *When you were taken, you were doing something Steve Dorsey should have done?*

That's right, came Nick's reply. *It was just busy-work, dropping something off at a messenger service. Dorsey made it sound like a big deal, though. Like I was doing something really meaningful for my father. You know, quality time.*

Amy wondered if Nick knew how clearly she could read the rest of what he was feeling.

You don't like Steve Dorsey, do you?

Nick's thoughts gave the equivalent of a snort of derisive laughter.

Actually, it's the other way around, he responded. *Dorsey doesn't like me. Doesn't like who and what I am. It interrupts his fantasy. Before I came along, he could pretend he was the son of the great Elmore Granger.*

"Miss Johnson?"

The world tilted without warning.

No, Amy thought, before she could help it. *No, not yet! I haven't learned enough.*

Amy, what is it? Nick asked sharply. *What's going on?*

"Miss Johnson," the voice said again. "Are you all right?"

What's happening? Nick's voice shouted. *Where are you? That's Dorsey's voice.*

Amy's eyes flew open.

Steve Dorsey's green eyes hovered above her. In slow motion, she watched him reach down to grasp her arm.

No, she thought. *No, don't.*

Amy! she heard Nick cry.

She felt Steve Dorsey's fingers close around her upper arm like a vise.

Amy screamed.

She felt her contact with Nick spike, as if he was struggling to hold on to her. Then it was cut off, as if severed by a knife. In its place, another image flooded Amy.

A wall of fire.

She could feel the air around her grow hot, as if she were standing near a blast furnace. Sobbing from a throat too dry to make a sound, Amy did the only thing she could do. The thing Brian Newcomb had done before her.

She lifted her hands to cover her eyes.

"Let go of her!" she heard a voice shout. She felt Steve Dorsey's hand being knocked away.

The fire vanished as abruptly as it had started. Amy toppled over. She wrapped her arms around herself, hugging her body as if to form her own straitjacket. But she kept her eyes closed.

"Amy," her father said. "Amy, can you hear me?"

He pulled her into his arms.

"Answer me, Amy," her father shouted. *"Can you hear me?"*

Somehow, she never knew how, Amy managed to nod.

"Get her a glass of water," she heard her father command Steve Dorsey. *"Do it now!"*

Amy felt a gust of air move by her as Steve Dorsey hurried off. She began to shiver uncontrollably.

Her father wrapped both arms around her, mimicking Amy's own. "It's all right, sweetheart," he soothed. "It will be all right now."

But it isn't, Dad, Amy thought. *I'm not sure it ever can be now.* Not now that the past was reaching out, seeking to destroy the future. And she was powerless to control it.

"I saw it, Dad," she choked out. "It was the fire. The fire from San Francisco."

fourteen

*A*my!

Nick surged up, his body reacting before he could stop it. His head knocked painfully against the top of his box. His feet kicked out against the bottom. He could feel the way his spontaneous actions made the whole coffin vibrate and shudder.

You'll kill yourself this way, he thought. And do his kidnapper's job for him.

He forced himself to lie still, taking in air in deep, slow gulps. But his heart still raced within the center of his chest. Something was wrong. She needed him. He was sure of it. And he had no way to help her.

Was this how she felt? he wondered. Trying to reach him. Trying to save him.

He tried to think back over the last few seconds of contact. What had she said? That his mind might hold details that were important? Details he didn't even know he had?

Could he figure out what happened to her, find a way to resume contact, if he only thought hard enough?

There was one thing he didn't need to think about. One thing he knew for certain, deep in his gut. Whatever trouble Amy was in, it had to do with Steve Dorsey.

Nick was certain it was Dorsey's voice he'd heard, calling out to Amy. For one disorienting second, he'd even sworn he could see him, see Dorsey's green eyes staring down.

Then everything had gone completely nuts, a cacophony of sensations so overpowering Nick couldn't hold on to Amy any longer. He'd lost her just when he was certain she needed him the most.

If anything happens to her, he realized, *I'll never forgive myself.* And realized with a shock that his fear for her had done the seemingly impossible.

It had driven out his fear for himself.

Nick lay in his box, the darkness all around him, the strange, new thought moving through his body.

It's true, he realized. *I'm not afraid anymore.*

He knew he still had plenty of reason to be afraid. His situation hadn't actually changed. He was still trapped inside a box that might yet turn out to be his coffin.

I know that, Nick thought. Knew even that Amy might be nothing more than a figment of his desperate imagination. That rather than face the terrible prospect of dying alone, he'd simply conjured up another presence.

But he didn't believe it. He believed she was as real as he was. What had she said? That they'd met before? He didn't understand what she meant. All he knew was that he felt drawn to her. He needed her.

Because of Amy, he wasn't alone. Against all logic, he wasn't afraid anymore. Because he had something to live for now. The moment he could reach out and touch Amy Johnson.

Alone in his wooden box, Nick closed his eyes. In his mind, he formed an image, like a magician conjuring out of smoke. The two of them together, hands clasped.

I will help you find me, Amy, he silently vowed. *And on the day that I am free, this image won't be just an illusion anymore.*

fifteen
♉

"*Okay,*" Carl said, *pushing away a plate that contained* the crusts of bread from his chicken salad sandwich.

The three team members were sitting in an outdoor café not far from Carl's Seattle office. Amy'd been unable to eat a bite of lunch, even though she knew she had to refuel her tired mind and body.

The trouble was, she simply couldn't bring herself to do it. In spite of the warmth of the summer sun on her back, shivers still radiated from the pit of Amy's stomach.

But it wasn't the cold of temperature, she thought. It was the cold of fear. The kind of fear that made her knees wobble and turned the marrow of her bones to ice.

The fear that what she'd just experienced meant history was going to repeat itself. Nick Granger was going to die. Because she was going to fail him.

Nausea rolled through Amy abruptly. Desperate to fight it back, she picked up her sandwich. She'd ordered peanut butter and jelly, for a big protein hit.

Eat, she told herself sternly. *You can't find Nick if you fold in the home stretch.*

She took a bite and chewed slowly. The peanut butter tasted like gooey sawdust in her mouth. She forced herself to take a second bite, then a third one. Then a sip of milk.

Drinking the cool liquid reminded her of the way Elmore Granger had suddenly appeared in Nick's room, carrying her drink of water, with a visibly upset Steve Dorsey trailing behind him.

Granger had been remarkably understanding about the whole episode, Amy thought. Though she was sure her condition must have been distressing to him, Amy had received nothing but sympathy and support from Nick's father.

He was overjoyed to hear she'd been able to contact Nick again. Sorry for both of them she hadn't been able to maintain the connection long enough to gather the additional information they all so desperately wanted.

He hadn't even probed into how or why the contact had been broken, much to Amy's relief, though his eyes had rested briefly on Steve Dorsey. Instead, he'd simply assured her that any part of his estate would be available to her any time she needed it.

His dark eyes burning down into hers, Granger had informed Amy she could have anything he could provide, if only it would help her locate Nick.

It had been her one glimpse beneath Elmore Granger's smooth, controlled surface. A view straight down into the fierce emotions that roiled beneath.

Elmore Granger was like a volcano waiting to erupt. Amy didn't think she wanted to be anywhere near the blast zone when he did.

Just thinking about the powerful emotions she'd seen in him made her shiver once more with fear. She could not fail. Not this time. She put her sandwich back down on her plate.

"So," Carl said, pulling Amy's thoughts back to the present. He picked up his glass of soda, took a sip, set it back down exactly in the same spot.

"Let me just make sure I've got this straight. You go into Nick's room. You find his favorite sweater. You put it on. You make contact, and everything is hunky-dory. Then Dorsey comes in, and all hell breaks loose."

Carl paused, his gaze shifting between Amy and her father. "Somebody here have an explanation?"

"I don't know," Amy exclaimed, her voice and her temper rising. "I don't know what happened, Carl. If I did, I'd tell you. And I'd do my best to make sure it didn't happen again, believe me. I have no desire to see those images. Ever."

"The images of the fire in San Francisco?"

Amy nodded, unwilling to trust her voice.

"And you've never seen them before now?"

Another shiver crept from the pit of Amy's stomach. Maybe the sandwich hadn't been such a good idea.

"Not during this case. Only in my nightmares," she answered, her voice low and ragged. "But I haven't had one of those in months." She glanced over at her father.

"We were kind of hoping..." Stan Johnson picked up, then halted.

Amy cleared her throat. "It's all right, Dad. You can say it," she said, her voice stronger. "We were hoping they were gone for good. That everything that happened to me after the Rising Dawn was finally over. I don't know what it means that I saw the fire again, Carl. I only know what I'm afraid of."

Carl looked across the table at her, compassion and concern written plainly on his face. Amy's father jiggled his glass, causing the ice cubes to rattle.

But neither of them asked her to name her fear, she noticed. Probably because they didn't have to.

"How are the rest of the water searches going?" Amy's dad asked, changing the subject.

Carl's face grew grim. "Not well," he answered shortly. "So far, we've come up with nothing on Lake Washington or Lake Union. Greenlake has pretty high foot traffic and not many structures right on the water. Without more details it's pretty hard to know where to focus."

Details, Amy thought. *That was supposed to be my job.*

But the only details she could provide weren't about what was threatening to destroy Nick Granger. They were about the thing that had almost destroyed her.

"We've assumed Nick's still in western Washington," Carl went on. "But let's face it, the kidnapper could have taken him east of the mountains for all we know. Hell, he could be in somebody's bathtub, for that matter. All it takes to drown someone is about two inches of water."

Amy took another sip of milk. "Thanks for that tidbit, Carl."

"Okay, look," Carl said suddenly, "let's try a different approach here. We're forgetting something positive happened this morning. I mean, before the fire thing, you made contact with Nick, right?"

Amy nodded. "Right," she said.

"So," Carl said, his voice and his eyebrows rising.

So I discovered we'd met before. That I think I'm in love with Nick and have been for months.

Amy's hand jerked at the answer her mind had produced, entirely without warning. Her glass tipped, then toppled over.

"Whoa," her dad said as milk cascaded toward him. Amy made a dive for the spill with her napkin. Caught it just in time.

Carl stood up to signal a passing server.

"Anybody ever told you you ought to do something about that drinking problem?"

"Happens all the time," the server assured Amy as she attacked the puddle of white liquid with a damp towel. "We have ways of dealing with people like you," she told Carl with a wink. "You want a refill on that, honey?"

Amy shook her head, her senses still swimming. "No, thank you," she replied.

"So," Carl prompted once again.

I can't tell them. I can't ever tell them, Amy thought in desperation. Her feelings for the guy she now knew was Nicholas Granger had to remain her secret, just the way they'd always been.

If her father knew she was emotionally connected to Nick, Amy was certain he'd yank her off the case so fast it would make her head spin. Being emotionally connected was dangerous. For her. For Nick. For them all.

Come on, Amy, she told herself. *Focus. Say something.*

"Actually," she said, thinking back, "there was something about Steve Dorsey. Remember how weird he was about the tour, Dad? How it felt like he was in this big hurry?"

"I remember," her father answered. "I also remember he didn't seem too wild about you spending time alone in Nick's room."

Amy nodded. "Well, in my contact with Nick, he told me the reason he went downtown was to run an errand for his father."

"What?" Carl said.

"He went downtown to run an errand," Amy repeated. "He dropped something off at a messenger service. When he was finished, he just kind of wandered around. But according to Nick, the person who was supposed to run that errand was Steve Dorsey."

Amy could feel both Carl and her father go completely still. Predators catching the scent.

81

"Say that one more time," Carl said slowly.

"Nick told me that Steve Dorsey sent him on that errand to the messenger service," Amy said. "He said Dorsey was supposed to do it and that he handed it off at the last minute."

Amy's father's head swiveled in Carl's direction. "When you interviewed Dorsey, did he tell you that?"

"He most certainly did not," Carl answered.

"There's something else," Amy said. "I got the distinct impression from Nick that he thought Dorsey didn't like him, was jealous of him, even. As if Nick's appearance had spoiled Dorsey's fantasy that he was Granger's son."

Carl gave a low whistle.

"That is definitely hot," he said.

For the first time since she'd seen those horrible images of the fire, Amy felt her tension lessen. Carl looked even more like a Volvo now. Amy could practically hear his engine revving.

"Dorsey could have gotten to Granger Senior any time," put in Amy's father quietly. "He's the one with greatest access."

"Yeah," Carl acknowledged. "So maybe we were wrong about this being a way to get Granger out in the open. Maybe it's just plain revenge. A way for Dorsey to get what he thinks is his fair share. He takes the money, like it's his inheritance or something, then quits his job and leaves the country."

Stan Johnson nodded vigorously. "Put a price tag on that and I'll buy it."

Amy rolled her eyes. "Dad, for crying out loud."

"Hey, just trying to sound like a cop in the movies," her father answered.

"So what now?" Amy asked.

Carl shut his notebook with a snap.

"First, I want to know more about that message

Nick delivered," he said. "Maybe it ties in somehow. And then I think it's time to do a little more digging. I want to know as much as possible about Mr. Steven Dorsey."

sixteen
♪

"*J*unk mail for Miss Amy Johnson," her father said at breakfast the next morning. He tossed a thick manila envelope down on the table.

Amy glanced at the legal-sized envelope. A clump of American flag stamps in the right-hand corner, no return address in the left. Her name typed across the front in big block letters.

Junk mail is right, she thought. The only people who didn't include a return address were the ones who were trying to sell you something.

"Why do they deliver this stuff first?" she commented.

Her father shrugged. "Because it's oversized, I guess," he said. "That way the postman doesn't have to carry it around all day."

He set the morning paper down beside his place at the table, then reached for the box of cereal. He began to pour himself a bowl, then stopped.

"How come you're eating this?" he asked. "You hate cold cereal."

Amy pointed to the box. "See what it says right there? 'Breakfast of Champions.' The way things are going, I figure I need all the help I can get."

Amy was so tired she almost couldn't see straight. Even simple actions took total concentration. She felt as if she were clinging to the edge of a cliff by her fingernails. One false move and she would lose her grip.

She was trying not to dwell on how Nick must be feeling after nearly three days in a box from which he might never have been intended to escape.

I have to find him, soon, she thought. *I have to focus.*

She scooted back from the table.

"Where are you going?" her father asked.

Amy picked up her mug, the largest she could find in the house. "More coffee."

Her father pushed his mug toward her. "Me, too," he said. Amy grunted.

I probably shouldn't have any more, she thought as she went into the kitchen and poured herself a fresh cup of coffee. The caffeine might help her stay awake, but it wasn't doing her nerves any good. They were already totally on overdrive, stretched thin and humming like a telephone wire.

Today was her last chance. If she couldn't find Nick Granger today, she would never find him.

She set the pot down on the counter with a clank and returned to the table with the two mugs of coffee.

Her father's blue eyes watched her over the handle of his spoonful of cereal. "You get any sleep at all?" he asked as Amy carefully set his coffee mug down in front of him.

Amy slid back into her own chair. "Huh uh," she said. She took a sip of coffee, jerking the cup back quickly as the hot liquid burned her tongue.

"Me neither," her dad said. "Not much."

"Well, I'm going to see the new gallery space this morning," her mother's voice sang out. "Wish me luck, everybody."

Amy started. She'd been so busy concentrating on

not burning her tongue she hadn't heard her mother come up behind her.

Amy's coffee cup tilted dangerously, then slipped. Coffee streamed out across the dining room table.

"Somebody rescue that envelope," Amy's mother said. "It's getting soaked."

Amy scooped up the envelope. Her father sprinted to the kitchen for a towel.

"Good luck, Mom," Amy said.

Her mother laughed. It was a good sound, Amy thought. She was glad there was someone in the house who could still laugh. Amy's father came back from the kitchen just as the doorbell started ringing.

"What is this, Grand Central Station?" said her mother.

"It's probably Carl," Amy's dad said.

"I'll let him in," said Rebecca Johnson. "Since I'm on my way out anyway. Stan . . ." she went on. Amy heard her parents move off through the living room, the low murmur of their voices. The sound of the front door opening.

While she waited, Amy tore open the back of the envelope. The soggy pieces stuck to her hands. Before she could prevent it, a jumble of papers spilled out onto the carpet.

Amy felt her heart kick against her chest. It pounded so loudly, she never heard the good-bye her mother called out to her. Never heard her father's and Carl's returning footsteps.

"I was right," her dad said, coming back into the dining room. "It's Carl."

"So," Carl said. "I hear you had another beverage incident."

"Amy, for God's sake," her father said as he caught sight of her face. "Honey, what is it?"

Unable to make her voice work, Amy simply

pointed. The pile of papers, mostly copies of newspaper clippings, lay face up at her feet.

"What the hell?" her father said. He moved to gather them up.

Amy's throat felt as if it were filled with ground glass. "Don't," she said. "Spread them out, Dad. Let Carl see. It could be important."

Without another word, Stan Johnson spread the clippings out until they all were visible. He didn't object to his daughter's request, but his mouth was set in a thin, hard line, and Amy could see that his hands were trembling.

Carl hunkered down beside him to get a closer look, then whistled through his teeth. "Oh, man."

The first clipping was a photo of the aftermath of a fire that had been more than a fire. This had been an inferno. One that had burned so hot it had taken everything it touched.

No victims' bodies left to mourn. Not even any bones to bury. The fire had been too greedy for that. It had taken all of them with it.

The next clipping was a reproduction of a school picture, a second grade class. Twenty-five young faces smiling or staring solemnly toward the camera. New school clothes crisp, hair slicked back. Taped alongside it was a copy of an individual student's photo. The name of the student was typed beneath the photograph in small letters.

Amy took a shuddering breath and stared into the eyes of the boy in the picture.

"Brian Newcomb," the black letters said.

There were clippings about the families of the students who'd been rescued, of tearful reunions.

And another photograph of the whole class, once again standing together, at Brian Newcomb's funeral. Their faces pale, eyes large as they stared at their classmate's small coffin, white as washed bone against the smooth green grass.

And finally there was a series of pictures of Amy. The images were grainy, as if the photos had been taken from a great distance and then blown up to make them large enough to see clearly.

Put together, they formed a sequence, like a scene in a movie. In it, Amy struggled against four uniformed police officers. She could see herself straining forward, mouth wide open, screaming in rage and agony.

She didn't remember the moment herself, but she remembered the bruises she'd found on her arms later. Knew from her father that, no matter how hard she'd pulled and screamed, the officers had refused to let her go.

Hadn't let her throw herself into the fire, trying to get to Brian Newcomb.

Somewhere, someone had collected the images from all her worst nightmares and sent them to her.

"Why?" she said. "I don't understand why."

"I think I know why," Carl said. "And who."

"Who?" Stan Johnson demanded, his voice tight with suppressed fury. He shifted position, sending the papers shooting across the floor, the images splintering like the jagged pieces of a kaleidoscope. "Tell me, Carl, who do you think did this?"

Carl shot a quick look at Amy. For the first time, Amy noticed how tired he looked. As if he hadn't gotten any more sleep than she had. He ran his hand across his face, a perfect imitation of her father's gesture.

"I think it's Steve Dorsey."

seventeen

$\mathscr{D}$

Amy's legs folded up. She sat back down on her chair at the table, heedless of the fact that it was damp with coffee.

"But why?" she asked. "I mean, I know we thought he might be involved in Nick's kidnapping, because of the messenger service thing. But why would he do this to me?"

"To distract you," her father said at once, getting to his feet. "Frighten you. Confuse you. Anything to make it harder for you to focus on Nick. To find him."

And it had worked, Amy thought, her hands turning to ice in terror. For the moments she'd stared at those pictures, the images of her own nightmares, for the space of time she'd stared into the face of her greatest failure, her greatest fear, nothing else had mattered.

She'd forgotten everything and everyone else. Including Nick Granger.

"It could also be something else," Carl said.

Amy's father moved to lean in the doorway between the living and dining rooms. He waited until Carl sat down across from Amy before he spoke.

"All right, Carl," he said, folding his arms across his chest. "How bad is it?"

Carl's head swiveled as he looked from father to daughter.

"You remember what we thought might be Dorsey's motive in the first place?" he asked.

"Sure." Amy spoke before her father could. "Some sort of twisted revenge. A way to prove to Elmore Granger that Dorsey's the one who should really be his son. That Granger never appreciated what he had."

"Well, now I think we're only partly right."

"Which part?" asked Amy's dad.

"The revenge," Carl said. "I'm just not so sure Elmore Granger is really the target."

He paused. A thick silence filled the air.

"I *don't* think Elmore Granger is the target," Carl repeated, more emphatically this time. "But I do think we were allowed, even led, to think he is."

"Which would mean the real target is . . ." Amy let her voice trail off.

"You, Amy," Carl said.

Amy felt her breath shoot from her lungs in shock. This was worse than a nightmare. If she was the target, then Nick had been taken because of her. Suffered because of her. His imprisonment was all her fault.

"You think he took Nick Granger because of me? Why?" she choked out.

"Because of what happened in San Francisco a year ago," Carl answered. "Because of the fire that killed the members of the Rising Dawn."

Amy shook her head, trying to assemble her scattered thoughts. "I just don't get it. I'm sorry, Carl. You mean because he blames me, like people blame the FBI for what happened at Waco?"

"Maybe," Carl answered. "Though I think it's more personal than that. After what happened to you yesterday, I did some more checking on Steve Dorsey. He was in San Francisco at the time of the fire."

Amy could feel a coldness settle in the pit of her stomach. "So were about a million other people."

"His sister was a cult member," Carl countered. "They had different last names, so finding the link took us a while. Part of the problem is that nobody has good information about the Rising Dawn members. Who they were. Where they came from. Only other cult members knew that.

"And none of the standard identification procedures worked after the fire. There wasn't enough left of the bodies to identify. We still don't really know how many cult members were in that compound or how many died. There could be cult members still alive that we don't know about."

"You're saying Dorsey could be a cult member, for all we know," Amy's dad put in.

Carl nodded. "I'm saying it's a strong possibility."

Amy shook her head, trying to clear her thoughts. "So why would he take Nick Granger? And why wait until now? My family didn't exactly hide where we were going when we left San Francisco. We've been here nearly a whole year."

"But Granger didn't move here until fairly recently," said Carl. "Maybe both our scenarios are right. Maybe Dorsey saw the opportunity to kill two birds with one stone. He gets revenge on Elmore Granger for what he sees as rejection, and you for the Rising Dawn."

"Not only that, Elmore Granger is the perfect decoy," Amy's father supplied. "Figuring we'd view Nick's kidnapping as a way to get to his father is a pretty safe bet."

"That's right," Carl agreed at once. "But what if it wasn't that at all? What if it was an attempt to get to Amy? To get her out into the open?"

"And then do what?" Amy asked, her throat suddenly as dry as dust.

"That," Carl said, "is what I'd like to know. If his motive is revenge, there's a good chance he means to harm you. Make you pay for the deaths in San Francisco. Maybe that accounts for the way you reacted when he touched you the other day. Maybe you were picking up on that."

He held his hand up as Amy opened her mouth to protest. "I know that's not the way your talent usually works," he said. "But nothing about the way it's working is quite usual on this case, is it?"

"So what do we do now?" Amy asked.

She watched as Carl and her father made quick eye contact, then ran their hands across their faces in perfect unison. Another time, she might have laughed. But not now. Not when she thought she knew what was coming.

"You tell her," Stan Johnson suggested.

"We take you off the case," Carl said.

Amy shot from her chair as if fired from a gun.

"No!" she said. "I won't give up on Nick. You can't ask me to do that."

"Amy," said her father, "be realistic, honey. If you're Dorsey's target, you could be in incredible danger."

"Nick's already in danger," Amy came back.

"I know that," her dad said. "I don't like it any better than you do."

"We know Dorsey's connected to the kidnapping," Carl spoke up. "Remember the package Nick told you about? We followed up on it. It bounced to services all over town before it finally reached its intended destination.

"That package was sent to Elmore Granger, Amy. Dorsey had Nick deliver his own ransom note. That's the kind of mind we're dealing with here. He's got more slippery curves than a snake. I want you off this case and somewhere safe."

"Where?" Amy demanded. "He knows where I live, Carl. He's been here. If he's gone to this much trouble, he won't give up just because I do."

"He'll have to," Carl said, "once we take him into custody. I've got enough now to pick him up."

"No!" Amy said again. "You can't do that, don't you see? If you're right about what he is, about him being a member of the Rising Dawn, he doesn't care about what happens to Nick. He won't ever tell you where he is."

Amy began to pace as her thoughts flowed more quickly. Finally, her brain was kicking into gear.

"Maybe that's his revenge, making me responsible for another death. Maybe he doesn't want to hurt me physically. But he won't be afraid to let Nick die, and you won't be able to make him tell you where Nick is because he isn't afraid of anything you can do to him."

"You can't know that," Carl countered.

Amy whirled toward him, stamping her foot in fury and frustration.

"Yes, I *can*," she cried. "You know about the Rising Dawn from what you've read. But I was there. I saw them in action.

"There is absolutely no doubt about how that fire in San Francisco started. *The cult members started it themselves*. They deliberately chose to die. They didn't care about their own lives or the lives of their hostages. *That's* the kind of mind we're dealing with here."

She stopped, her fury vanishing as one crystal-clear thought took hold and began to grow.

"Oh, God."

"What?" her father demanded at once, moving swiftly to her side.

"Wait a minute," Amy said. "Nobody move. Everybody just stand still and be quiet."

She could feel the stillness deep inside her, spreading, growing strong.

"He's doing it again," she said. "What was it you said, Carl? More slippery curves than a snake?"

"He's doing what again?" Carl barked.

"Distracting us," Amy said. "The clippings of the fire. Letting us think he wants revenge against Elmore Granger. The ransom note bouncing all over town. They're all the same thing. He's distracting us. Trying to make us lose our focus. Twisting us around."

"Well, it's working," Amy's dad said shortly.

"Yes," Amy said. "But what if we're not the only ones? What if that's exactly what he did with Nick by putting him underwater? What if he deliberately chose the thing Nick was afraid of most, knowing his fear would distract him, become *his* only focus?"

Carl's eyebrows rose. "I suppose that's possible."

"Don't you see we have to find Nick?" Amy asked urgently. "It's the best way to ensure that I'll be safe. The only way to beat Steve Dorsey. Let me go back to Nick's room. Contact him once more, where our connection is the strongest.

"If I can get him to filter out his fear, I can get to the details that can save him. Save us both."

"And if you can't?" her father asked quietly.

"I have to try again, Dad," Amy said. "Failure is no longer an option. All I've done is focus on failure, my fear of it, for a whole year. You know that better than anyone. But all of a sudden, just now, I realized something else."

Looking up into her father's eyes, Amy was startled to discover they had tears in them.

"What did you realize, sweetheart?" asked her father softly. "I think I know what it is, but I want to hear you tell me that *you* know it."

"I didn't fail that day in San Francisco."

Amy's father rubbed a hand across his eyes.

94

"I got twenty-four kids out of that compound," Amy continued. "Twenty-four of them, alive. Brian Newcomb wasn't one of them, and I'm never going to be able to forget that. I'll live with that for the rest of my life. But he didn't die because I failed him, Dad. Brian Newcomb died because he was afraid.

"He let his fear distract him. Rule him. For a year, I've let mine do the same. Well, I'm not going to let my fear run me any longer. Starting right now. Today. I know myself now, Dad. I know my own strength. And because I do, I'm going back to Nick's room for one more contact. I'm going to find him, and absolutely nothing is going to distract or stop me."

Amy felt her father's arms surround her. "I love you, Amy. I believe that you can do what you believe you can. I always have."

"So," Amy said against her father's chest, "does this mean you're coming with me?" She felt his laughter rumble against her cheek.

"Carl?" he asked.

"Only if I can come along, too," Carl answered. Amy lifted her head. Carl's face still looked exhausted, but his eyes had spark again.

"I was hoping you'd say that," she answered.

"Then let's do it," Carl said. "The clock is still running, people."

Amy stepped back, out of the shelter of her father's arms.

"You know . . ." Carl said.

"What?" Amy asked.

"I came here convinced we'd lost Nick Granger. Now I wouldn't give a nickel for Steve Dorsey's chances."

Amy actually grinned.

"Let's see if we can turn the tables on him, distract him for a change," she said. "Granger said the house

95

and grounds were available to us anytime, right? So let's just show up. Don't call ahead.''

Carl nodded. "Good suggestion," he said. "Let's see if we can force Dorsey to lose his focus, make a mistake. As far as I'm concerned, it's time somebody started messing with *his* head.''

eighteen
18

He was almost out of time.

The air in the box felt hot and stuffy, as if the supply from outside were being slowly shut down.

The water was gone. His lips were chapped, his throat dry, his tongue thick and gummy.

Now that the water was gone, he realized how hungry he was. No food at all since they'd put him in the box. Only air. Only water. Enough to keep him going for just so long. But no longer.

The hunger made his stomach twist into a hard knot, made his body heavy and his head strangely light. As if it could float to the top of the box and bob there, like a fishing lure.

How long? he wondered. How long before whoever had taken him decided to drown him? Before he let in the water?

He'd always been certain that was how this would end. Not with suffocation. But with drowning. His life had never been quite like other people's. So why should his death be any different?

He was going to die here, drowned in this box like the victim of some demented magic trick.

Unless the miracle he was still hoping for could happen. Unless Amy could find him.

But there'd been no contact with her for what felt

like hours upon agonizing hours. What was happening? Where was she?

Finally, he'd forced himself to face the truth, the inevitable conclusion. She wasn't coming back for him. Couldn't save him. Because his fevered brain had made her up. She'd never existed in the first place.

It had been the darkest moment in his dark night of the soul. The one from which he feared there would be no awakening.

But then, when he'd least expected it, he'd seen the flare of light. Like the big bang that had brought the universe into existence, he'd seen the bursting into existence of his own hope.

He wouldn't give up. Wouldn't ever give up. And neither would Amy. She was out there, somewhere. Searching. As long as he drew breath, he would believe that.

Trust that she would not leave him to die alone in this place. Believe that she would keep her promise.

Because, with a certainty no fear, despair, or logic could shake, Nick Granger believed that Amy Johnson existed.

And that she would yet be his salvation.

nineteen
D

The ride to the Granger compound was accomplished in almost total silence. Amy stared at the back of Carl's and her father's heads from her position in the backseat of Carl's unmarked police car.

Even as she watched his body sway through the twists and turns of the road that led to Elmore Granger's house, Amy could tell by the set of her father's neck and shoulders that he was tense and worried. And Carl's shoulders were practically attached to his earlobes.

Amy was sure her body language mirrored theirs. If she couldn't find Nick now, she never would. This was going to be their, *her*, last chance.

She set her hand down on the seat next to her, her fingers just brushing a letter-sized envelope with Nick's watch inside. At Amy's request, Carl had placed the watch in the envelope, then carried it to the car with a pair of kitchen tongs.

Amy wanted the watch with her when she reached Nick's room, but no contact with it before. She also didn't want anyone else to touch it, not after what had happened yesterday with Steve Dorsey.

Strangely enough, now that she'd had time to absorb it, Carl's news of this morning was actually making Amy feel better. As if his discovery that Dorsey had connections to the Rising Dawn—and might even be a cult member—had shifted the burden for the images she'd seen when he'd touched her, from her to him somehow.

The images of the fire that had so frightened and overwhelmed her hadn't been Amy's past catching up with her. They'd come from Steve Dorsey himself.

All the more reason for me not to be afraid anymore. To trust myself, she thought. The stronger her trust in her own talent, the greater her chances to find Nick.

"Gates coming up," Carl murmured. "We're all clear about the way we do this, right? We get in, Amy goes directly to Nick's room without stopping. Do not pass go, do not collect two hundred dollars."

"What about Steve Dorsey?" Amy asked.

She caught Carl's grim expression in the rearview mirror. "I'll collect Steve Dorsey," he said.

He rolled down the window. "Detective Carlson, Mr. and Miss Johnson to see Mr. Granger," he told the approaching security guard.

"I'll need to see your ID," the guard said. Carl's badge flashed in the sun as he held it out. "Very good, Detective. Mr. Granger's orders are that you be admitted at any time. If you'll just wait a moment, while I open the gate."

"Sure thing," said Carl.

Amy clutched the corner of the envelope while she waited for the gate to open.

She heard the sharp metallic *click* as the lock released, the high-pitched electronic whine as the gate swung open. Finally, the crunch of leaves as it came to a halt against the prickly hedge flanking the entrance.

All things her heightened sense recorded now, when, on her first visit, she'd been too preoccupied to notice them.

"Go on through," the guard instructed.

"Thanks," Amy's dad said.

Amy saw his eyes move to the sideview mirror. "He's on the walkie-talkie now," he said.

"So now Dorsey knows we're coming," Carl answered. "Let's hope he doesn't know whether to gloat or sweat."

They completed the final curve before the drive. Carl's eyes met Amy's in the rearview mirror.

"All set?"

"Ready as I'll ever be," Amy said.

Carl pulled the car up in front of the house just as Steve Dorsey bounded down the front steps.

"The gate just called to alert me of your presence, Detective. This is most unexpected. I'm sure Mr. Granger will be most alarmed at the precipitous nature of your visit. It would have been much better if you'd phoned ahead."

"I'm sure he'll be more alarmed if we don't find his son, Mr. Dorsey," Carl answered. He got out of the car and shut it with a slam. He nodded at Amy as she emerged from the backseat. "All right, Amy. Go ahead."

Steve Dorsey's head swiveled in Amy's direction. "Now, wait just a minute," he protested. "Go ahead where?"

"Mr. Granger made his property available to us whenever we felt we needed it, Mr. Dorsey," Amy's father said almost conversationally as Amy moved toward the front steps.

But her father kept himself between her and Dorsey, Amy noticed. So there was no way he could get his slimy hands on her. Carl stepped up on the other side, so that he, Dorsey, and Amy's father formed a triangle where Dorsey was outflanked.

"And we feel we need to have it available to us now," Carl said.

"Well, yes, of course, I realize that," Steve Dorsey blustered. "But I'm quite sure that what Mr. Granger meant—"

"Thank you, Steve," said a voice behind him. Amy skidded to a halt. Elmore Granger stood in the doorway, his form blocking the entrance to the house.

"Much as I appreciate your attention to detail," he continued. "I don't require you to explain to the detective what I meant. I think it's quite clear, in fact. 'Available whenever necessary' means just that."

Steve Dorsey's mouth opened and closed rapidly, like a fish out of water. Amy half expected him to start gasping for breath.

"My dear," Elmore Granger said, switching his attention to Amy. He took a step toward her, his eyes bright and piercing as a laser. "May I hope that this visit means you know where my son is?"

"We can both hope that, Mr. Granger," Amy answered. Her heart was hammering so hard she was sure it was visible through the thin cotton of her shirt. She struggled to battle back a wave of fear.

How would she face him after this if she couldn't find Nick?

I will not be afraid anymore, she vowed. *I will not be distracted or ruled by my fear.* She lifted her chin.

"If I could just have a little more time in Nick's room," she said. "Alone and undisturbed."

"Of course," Elmore Granger said at once. "I don't know why we're wasting time out here. You go up. I'll stay with your father and Detective Carlson."

Granger's eyes rested on the pale face of his assistant for just a moment. "And, of course, with you, too, Steve. Hurry, now," he went on, switching his attention back to Amy. "I want my son back, Miss Johnson. I'll see to it that you're not disturbed."

As he spoke, Elmore Granger stepped clear of the doorway. Amy sprinted across the entry hall and up the stairs. The door to Nick's room was standing open. The burgundy sweater was spread out on the bed.

As if his father had left it out for him. *A good luck token,* Amy thought.

She yanked the sweater on with one swift motion, then sat on Nick's bed. With trembling fingers, she tore open the envelope and tipped the watch out, slipping it onto her wrist.

Come on, Nick, she prayed silently. *Be there.*

This time the motion toward contact was like moving through wet cement. Amy's slip through different layers of consciousness was slow and sluggish, as if dictated by Nick's diminishing strength.

Let me be in time, she thought. *Please, let me be in time.*

Can you hear me? she sent. *Can you hear me? It's Amy, Nick.*

Amy, she heard his thought come back. But it was fuzzy, out of focus, lacking strength. *I knew it,* she heard him say. *Knew I didn't dream you up. I knew that you'd come back. You promised me I wouldn't die alone, and now I won't.*

I'm in your room, Nick, Amy sent. Anything to keep him engaged, she thought. To get him focused. *I'm wearing your favorite sweater. The burgundy one.*

She could feel a quick spurt of pleasure sweep through him, momentarily giving him energy.

That is *my favorite sweater,* Nick sent back.

Who made it for you? Amy asked. She knew, but she wanted to keep Nick engaged. Wanted to keep his energy up.

Pat's mom.

Pat. That's the guy you stained the deck with?

That's right, Nick said. Amy felt another spurt of energy. *How did you know about him?*

Amy could feel her excitement rising. He wasn't

too far gone. She could still make this work.

There's a picture in your room. But even before I saw that, I picked Pat up from your mind, Nick. The very first time that we made contact. I just saw an image, like I was watching a scene from a movie.

Interesting, Nick replied.

Nick, Amy thought quickly, *will you do something for me?*

Anything, Nick thought back, the wave of energy the greatest yet.

I want you to stop thinking about anything specific. I want you to just let your mind drift. Let it conjure up its own pictures. Try to show me the day you were kidnapped.

But I don't remember, Nick protested.

Maybe not consciously, Amy said. *Remember, we talked about this before? But you weren't consciously thinking about staining the deck with Pat. You just made an association and the image popped into your head. That's what I want you to do again.*

If you say so.

But Amy could feel the weariness seeping through him. Felt her pulse jolt up a notch in response. As if she was trying to give him her energy. To convince him that he could do this, that he could go on.

Somewhere in Nick's mind were the details that could save him. He might not believe it. But she did.

Come on, Nick. You can do this. Come on.

Okay, she said. *Just drift and let the pictures form in your mind. You've dropped off the package for your father. Now what are you doing? Show me the movie, Nick.*

A jumble of images flooded Amy's mind as Nick free-associated. But they were blurry around the edges, like old and out-of-focus photographs.

Amy became aware that her fingers were wrapped so tightly around the wrist wearing Nick's watch that she'd cut off the circulation to her hand.

She forced herself to relax, to send Nick a constant flow of steady energy. As if in response, the flood of images slowed, became sequential, took on greater focus.

And Amy felt their minds slide together, until she and Nick were completely one.

With one body, they walked through downtown Seattle. Staring up at the tall buildings from the hot, gray sidewalks. Up and down the streets, wandering aimlessly. Past Nike Town. Planet Hollywood. Coming to a halt at a crosswalk. Hearing the nearby noise of new construction.

As if in slow motion, Amy saw the shadow spreading slowly out into the crosswalk beside her. The hand that materialized in front of her face without warning. Crosswalk, pavement, buildings, all wheeled around her.

Before she could stop herself, Amy jerked back. Their shared consciousness splintered, became two separate minds once more. She saw one final image, of a sidewalk covered like a wooden bridge to protect it from the new construction before everything went abruptly black.

That's where they took you, Nick, she thought.

Where they could pull him out of sight beneath the temporary sidewalk cover. Mask whatever cry he might make with the confusion of the noise of new construction.

That's all. That's all I can remember, Nick thought in desperation.

No, it isn't, Amy came back, just as strong.

It couldn't be. It mustn't be. There had to be more. There had to be enough for her to save him. To find out where he was.

Okay, Nick, Amy thought. *We did this once. We can do it again. Just take a deep breath and let your mind go. When you woke up, it was dark, right?*

Yes, Nick answered. Amy could feel him begin to calm down.

And that's when you smelled the varnish?

Amy could practically feel him inhale. Trying to help his mind remember what his body had already experienced. She knew the moment he made the realization. His excitement hit her like a blow.

No, he said. *It was later. That must mean I woke up before they put me in the box, then blacked out again.*

That's great, Nick, Amy thought. *I know you can't see, but there must have been other sensations. Can you hear something? Smell anything?*

She felt it then. The thing she hadn't felt in days. Had never felt before in any of their contacts. And because of that, she had never even realized it had been missing.

Hope. Nick's hope. For the very first time, he believed that he might make it.

My stomach hurts, Nick said. *It feels queasy. It could be whatever they used to knock me out, but I think it's something more. I think it's because I'm . . . swaying. I used to get carsick on trips when I was little. Both my parents used to hate it. That's what my stomach feels like now.*

All right, so you could be traveling. Are you going fast? Stopping and starting like you're in traffic?

No, Nick answered. *But there's a lot of swaying. Like the road has twists and turns. Wait a minute, now we're stopping. I can't tell what for. There's this funny sound, like somebody walking through a pile of dried leaves. Now we're moving on, but more slowly.*

Amy could feel her whole body tingle. She closed her eyes, the better to concentrate on the sensations Nick's words were creating.

Like this, Nick? she thought.

And felt her body sway from side to side.

Yes, she heard Nick say. *That's it.*

She felt the motion stop. Heard the strange, high-pitched electric whine.

That was there, too, she heard Nick's voice exclaim excitedly. *You're right. I remember now.*

The crunch that sounded like dry leaves in the autumn.

Yes! Nick cried. *You know. You know. Where are we?*

Amy opened her eyes.

This was the thing Nick's kidnapper didn't want him to remember. The thing he'd taken such pains to distract him from, to cover up. If she hadn't just experienced it herself, she might never have made the connection.

They were starting down Nick's own driveway, through the open gates of the Granger compound.

But how is that possible? she heard Nick's voice inside her mind. *That can't be possible. It would mean that, all this time—*

Steve Dorsey hadn't concealed Nick in some remote location. He'd hidden him in plain sight. At home.

But where? Amy thought, struggling to find some corner of her mind that could still function on its own.

She knew the police had searched the lake shore. It was the first thing Carl had ordered done. There wasn't any other water on the property.

Water. Water. Water, Amy thought as she let her own mind free-associate. *Home. Home. Home.*

Images spun before her eyes, her own film, on fast forward. She heard Steve Dorsey's voice, whining like an insect as he extolled the virtues of the Granger estate, then slowing so that one sentence rang clear in Amy's head.

"Mr. Granger felt it was appropriate for Nick to confront his fears," Steve Dorsey said.

And Amy felt the final piece of the puzzle slide into place.

She vaulted from the bed like it was electrified and she'd just taken a thousand straight volts, and started running for the bedroom door.

"Dad," she screamed. "Dad, Carl. I know. I know."

She heard the front door bang back. The sound of feet pounding across the entry hall.

Hold on, Nick, Amy sent. *I'm coming. Hold on.*

She raced down the stairs, taking them two at a time.

"Amy." Her father reached out and brought her to a skidding halt as she reached the bottom. The second he touched her, her contact with Nick cut off.

But she was sure now. Sure she could save him. Sure she knew exactly where he was.

"Where, Amy?" her dad said.

"The lap pool, Dad," she choked out. "He's in the lap pool."

twenty

♪

For the rest of her life, Amy was sure she would remember this moment. The way the whole world seemed to pause, stop spinning at the sound of her voice.

Her father, staring down at her, his blue eyes dilated in shocked surprise. Behind him, Elmore Granger frozen in the open doorway.

Then Carl moved, and the world began to turn again as he spun around to put his hand on Steve Dorsey's shoulder. Dorsey jumped like he'd been prodded by a hot poker.

"What is the meaning of this?" he shouted.

Carl ignored him. "Go," he told Amy and her father. "I'll call for backup and hold on to Dorsey. It'll take me a moment to read him his rights."

He tossed his keys in a high arc to Amy's father. "There's a crowbar in the trunk. Get it. Hurry."

Elmore Granger stepped back. Amy catapulted through the doorway with her father right behind her. Stan Johnson sprinted for the car, but Amy was already starting down the path, the nutshells crackling beneath her feet.

"Amy, wait for me," her father yelled. Amy kept right on running.

Down the path with its tall, obscuring hedges. Past the outdoor tennis courts with their battery of surveillance cameras. If she and the police had played the tapes from those cameras back, would they have revealed the truth, or had Steve Dorsey altered them?

Past the gym her father had toured. To the one building Steve Dorsey hadn't let them go into. The lap pool, which he'd claimed was still under construction.

Amy skidded down the path toward it, her breath burning in her lungs. She reached for the door. Tugged. Found it locked.

"Nick," she screamed. "Hold on. We're coming."

"Amy, get back," she heard her father's voice command sharply. She skittered backward, moving to stand beside Elmore Granger. She watched as her father thrust the crowbar between the doorjamb and the door itself. The new wood shrieked as he pushed against it.

Once. Twice. Three times her father pushed, while the wood wailed like a banshee. And then the door cracked open on its hinges and Amy was inside the building.

It was dark inside the pool house after the brightness of the summer morning. Amy blinked, desperately trying to adjust her eyes, just as the beam of a flashlight snapped on behind her. Elmore Granger.

He played the light over the walls, then onto the surface of the floor in front of her. It was rough, uneven, unfinished.

"Watch your step," he said in a low voice. "I want to find him as much as you do, but don't hurt yourself in the process. Go slowly."

With the flashlight beam playing ahead of her, Amy forced herself to walk slowly forward. Until her toes extended out into space above the empty lap pool.

Then Nick's father directed the beam down into the pool itself. And Amy saw it wasn't really empty after all.

The bottom of the lap pool was covered with what a line on the side to mark the depth told them was a little more than four feet of water.

Just four feet. Not even as deep as Amy was tall. But more than enough to drown Nick. Just staring at the surface of the water made Amy's chest tighten.

Beside her, she heard Nick's father catch his breath. "Sweet merciful heaven," he whispered.

In the next instant, Amy's own father joined them, in his hands a second flashlight. He played it over the sides of the pool.

"There," he said, pointing with the beam.

In the far corner of the lap pool, a rope ladder descended into darkness. Elmore Granger shone his flashlight down along the ladder's length to where it disappeared beneath the surface of the water. A thin rubber tube ran along beside it.

Amy's father's voice was tight as he said, "That must be the air supply."

Abruptly, the doorway behind them darkened.

"Where is he?" Carl's voice barked. "Have you got him?"

Amy's dad flicked his light to show the location. "In the corner. We'll need help to get the box open."

A battery of lights exploded all around Amy as the backup team spread out around the pool. She heard a splash as the first officer went into the water.

"Give me your flashlight, Dad," she said. Before he could answer, she reached out and snatched it from him.

"Amy," her dad said sharply, "what are you doing?"

"I'm the one he feels the most connected to," she said, heedless of the fact that Nick's father stood right next to her. "I'm going down for him."

"*Amy,*" cried her father.

But she was already hurrying around the side of the

111

pool to where the rope ladder dangled down.

She sat down on the edge of the pool, tucked the flashlight beneath her chin, grasped the rope ladder with both hands, flung her legs out into space, and turned around. Her feet found the first rung of the ladder just as she heard the first shriek of wood from down below.

There were going to get the box open before she could get there.

"No!" Amy screamed, even though the officers underwater couldn't hear her. The flashlight slipped from beneath her chin and splashed into the water. "You don't understand what will happen. What he's going through. He's been alone for nearly three days. He's exhausted and terrified."

Especially terrified of the water.

A second shriek followed the first as the second crowbar was inserted. And Amy knew, if she continued as she was, she was never going to get there in time. She kicked free of the rope ladder, and dropped like a stone into the water.

There was water in his box.

Nick could feel it streaming down the sides of the coffin, soaking through the back of his clothes.

The part of his mind that still, just barely, functioned wondered how long it would take for the box that had been his prison to fill with water.

Amy! he thought. *Where are you? We came so close. So close.*

He heard a third shriek, like a demon screaming bloody murder. Water poured over him with a great rush.

And Nick Granger began to fight for his life.

His arms shot straight upward, striking the top of

the box. It emitted a final shriek and gave way. Nick surged upright.

Water was everywhere. Stinging his dry and aching eyes. Filling up his nose and mouth. He choked, and felt strong arms reach to hold him.

No, he thought. *I won't let you take me again. I won't let you hold me down.*

He struggled, lashing out wildly.

"Nick," he heard a voice shout. "Nick, stop it. You're all right."

But he didn't stop, couldn't make himself stop, until he felt a new set of hands, different from the others. They grasped him on either side of his face, held his head still.

And Nick knew, beyond a shadow of a doubt, that he was safe. The miracle had happened. His long ordeal was over.

Slowly, he opened his eyes. Looked down into a girl's face, beautiful even in the harsh glare of flashlights. Into a pair of eyes an impossible shade of blue.

"Nick, it's all right. It's Amy," she said.

"Amy?" he whispered.

But I know you.

From a day in San Francisco that seemed so long ago it was in a different lifetime now. A day he'd finally grown tired of sitting around waiting for the father who'd been so eager to have him, yet could never spare him any time. The day he'd struck out on his own.

He'd never felt so lonely in his life. Until he'd found the girl who seemed even lonelier than he was. Talking with her was the first time anyone but Pat had understood him. The last time he'd been happy. Until now.

He lifted one arm, his fingers brushing against her

cheek as if to assure himself that she was as real as he was.

"Amy," he whispered. "It's you."

Then he pitched forward into her arms.

twenty-one

Hours later, Amy sat at Nick's hospital bedside, watching as he slept. She knew she couldn't stay much longer. She was about to drop with weariness herself. But she wasn't quite ready to leave him yet.

The doctors had pronounced Nick fit but weakened from his three days without food and with only limited water. He needed a period of adjustment, a period of rest.

They'd hooked him up to an IV, which was providing vital fluids and nutrients. The bag, with its clear tubes of liquid stretching down to reach his arm, dangled from a stand above Amy's head. A battery of monitors, all silently pulsing green or red lights, filled a cart beside the bed.

Nick stirred, and one array of lights spiked silently. *Talk about wired for sound,* Amy thought. *Now everybody knows where you are, Nick.*

"How is he?" asked a voice from the doorway. Amy knew who it was without even turning her head. No one in the world had a voice like Elmore Granger.

"Still sleeping," she said. Elmore Granger crossed the room to sit in a second chair on the far side of the bed.

Nick's father looked completely exhausted. But as he looked at his son, his eyes glowed warmly.

"I still can't quite believe it," he said. He looked up, his dark gaze focusing intently on Amy. "And I don't believe I've truly thanked you yet, Miss Johnson. You have no idea what this means to me."

Amy shifted, made slightly uncomfortable by the intensity of Nick's father's scrutiny. "It was nothing, Mr. Granger," she protested, and felt the ridiculousness of the statement even as the words left her mouth.

Trying to save Nick hadn't been nothing. Accomplishing it had taken all she had. But the reward had been something she'd never imagined. Not just Nick's life, his safety. But the fulfillment of the most cherished dream Amy'd ever had.

"I'm sure anyone would have done it," she fumbled.

"Anyone who *could* have," corrected Elmore Granger. "But then that's just the point, isn't it? Not everybody could have done this. You were the only one who could, Miss Johnson."

"Please," Amy said. "My name is Amy."

The expression on Nick's father's face finally lightened. "Very well, Amy," he said. "And you must call me Elmore." His gaze shifted to rest upon his sleeping son's face.

"Something tells me it's appropriate for you and I to be on a more informal basis," Elmore Granger continued. "I have a feeling we'll be seeing more of one another."

He stood up before Amy could even begin to frame an answer.

"I'm afraid I must be going now," he said. "I hate to do it, but I'm an old man and I am tired. I know I leave him in good hands. Don't wear yourself out, though, my dear. Nick is safe now. There are plenty of people here to watch over him."

Elmore Granger crossed to the door. For a moment

Amy thought he would come to her, embrace her even, but at the last moment, he held back.

"Good night," Elmore Granger said. "And Amy—" He paused for a moment, as if struggling to find the right words. "I'm sorry about what happened with Steve Dorsey."

"Mr. Granger—" Amy protested.

He held up a hand, interrupting her. "Elmore," he said.

"Elmore," Amy corrected herself. It didn't really make a difference what she called him, she thought. She still couldn't believe what he was saying.

"How can you even think of apologizing for Steve Dorsey?" she asked. "You didn't know what he was. Even the police almost didn't find out until it was too late."

"But I brought him into my house," Nick's father said grimly. "I employed him. I should have made it my business to learn what he was. When I think what he did to Nick. The way he threatened you . . ."

"Please," Amy said, rising and crossing to him. She moved to put a hand on his arm, but Elmore Granger shifted position at exactly the same moment. Amy's arm dropped.

"You mustn't be concerned about what happened to me. It was nothing."

"Nothing," Elmore Granger repeated, his voice tinged with bitterness. "It is good of you to say so, but I wouldn't exactly call it that."

By the time Nick had been brought up from the pool, Steve Dorsey had been formally arrested. He'd sat, handcuffed, in a chair in the Granger entry hall, surrounded by police officers.

Amy had been astonished at the change in him. Being arrested for Nick's kidnapping had finally taken the edge off Steve Dorsey. No longer was he a sharp young business executive. He looked almost childlike in his dazed dismay.

But still, his eyes had followed Elmore Granger. As if, even now, Dorsey needed Granger's attention and approval. Needed to prove to himself that he was important to him.

All that had changed when he'd caught sight of Amy.

The sight of Amy had restored Steve Dorsey to his former self briefly, made his green eyes flash. He'd actually lunged for her, the officers pulling him back.

"You think you've won, don't you?" Dorsey had said. And Amy had been appalled to find herself fighting back a wild desire to laugh.

It was so exactly what the bad guy was supposed to say to take away the good guy's triumph. As if Steve Dorsey was still trying to pull the strings, create the script. As if he couldn't admit that it was over. His next words only served to highlight Amy's impression.

"You think it's over now, that this stops here," Steve Dorsey said. "Well, you're wrong, Miss Amy Johnson. Someday you're going to find out just how much. And on that day, I want you to know that, wherever I am, I'll know I've won. And I'll be laughing at you."

"Steve!" Elmore Granger's sharp voice had sliced across the entry hall. Dorsey's head had jerked in his direction. And then his face had crumpled. As if, even surrounded by the police, on his way to prison, a rebuke from Granger was still the worst thing that could possibly happen to him.

"I'm sorry," he whimpered. "I'm sorry. I'm so sorry."

Elmore Granger had turned away, leaving Steve Dorsey sobbing.

"Get him out of here," Carl had said, his voice tight.

And then the ambulance had arrived and, in accompanying Nick and his father to the hospital, Amy had forgotten all about Steve Dorsey. As far as she was concerned, Nick's father should, too.

"It's over now, Elmore," she said. "And, believe it or not, I've actually been threatened by much scarier people than Steve Dorsey."

Granger tilted his head, his dark eyes kindling as he looked at her. "What a remarkable young woman you are, Amy. I know it was you who found my son, but I think the truth is both my son and I are lucky to have found you."

Then he whirled and was gone, his hard-soled shoes clicking against the polished hospital floor, leaving Amy staring after him.

A rustle of bedclothes brought her attention back to Nick. Amy eased into her seat beside him just as his eyes opened.

Wide and dark, she thought, just like his father's. But, unlike his father's, full of fear. As if he couldn't quite remember where he was. That he was safe.

"It's all right, Nick," Amy said quickly, before his fear could mount. "You're safe. You're in the hospital. I'm right here."

His dark eyes focused upward onto hers, then roamed to search her face. *Amy.* His mouth formed the one word, though it made no sound. He cleared his throat. Tried again.

"Amy?"

His voice was rough with fatigue. Amy nodded, reaching for his hand. Wild sensations cascaded through her as their fingers met. Relief. Longing. Fear. But whether it was fear of what was happening between them now, or the memories of what he'd just experienced, Amy couldn't tell.

"Don't," Nick said. Heart shuddering, Amy pulled her fingers back. And felt his move to capture them again.

"Don't leave me yet," Nick said. Amy dropped her head to lean it against the metal railing of the bed. She didn't want him to see the way she'd misunderstood. How close she was to the razor's edge of tears.

She heard the bedclothes move once more. Felt Nick's fingers move against her face. He eased her chin up, staring straight into her tear-filled eyes.

"Don't, Amy," he said again. And ran his hand across her face to wipe her tears away. Amy leaned her cheek into his palm. He cradled it there.

"You're real," he said. "I didn't make you up. You're not a dream."

"No, Nick," Amy answered, her lips against his hand. "I'm not a dream."

And neither is what we share, she thought. She lowered his hand to the bedclothes, embracing it between both her own until he slipped at last into a deep and healing sleep.

twenty-two
D

The next few weeks passed peacefully, easily. The long, hot days of summer in full swing. Amy spent her time at home sketching plans for a new flower garden her father wanted to plant for her mother, or in the chic shopping area by the waterfront helping her mother ready the new gallery.

Amy'd never taken much part in the gallery her mom had run in San Francisco, although she'd been proud of her mother's accomplishments. Rebecca Johnson's work had always been somewhat separate from Amy and her father, just as she herself was in many ways.

Now, as Amy helped her mother review artist portfolios, paint walls, arrange display shelves, she felt a new closeness spring up between them, though she didn't fool herself into thinking everything was resolved. That would definitely take more than a coat of fresh paint.

But it was plain that both she and her mother were making an effort to start over, to learn about one another, to meet as friends.

Even Amy's dad came down to help, on leave from the police department. Offering hilarious and totally impractical suggestions such as purple paint for the gallery walls.

But every day, even as Amy rejoiced in the new-found closeness within her family, she couldn't stop thinking about Nick Granger.

They'd met several times since Nick's release from the hospital. Amy knew that, in many ways, Nick was doing the same thing she was. Spending time at home with his father, trying to forge the links that made a family.

In their own time together they'd done simple things. Easy things. The sort of things any new friends might do together. They'd gone for coffee, to a movie, ridden on the ferry.

For Amy, each experience was like holding a diamond ring up to the sunlight. Each time, it sparkled more brightly as she discovered some new facet. And Nick, tentative at first, had grown more and more comfortable and at ease.

There was only one thing to mar Amy's happiness. Not since those first moments in the hospital when he'd clung to her hand so tightly had Nick touched her.

Amy'd thought she was imagining things at first. The way he sat across the aisle from her if they rode the bus, across the table when they went for coffee.

It wasn't until he'd actually purchased two separate bags of popcorn at the movies that Amy admitted the truth. He'd done it so their hands wouldn't accidentally meet if they reached for the salty kernels at the same time.

He didn't want to touch her.

She was glad the movie theater was dark, glad the film turned out to be a tear-jerker. It meant she didn't have to explain the sudden lump in her throat or the way her eyes watered.

And it meant she could focus on the movie instead of on the horrible question looming in the back of her brain.

What would she do if, after finding him so unex-
pectedly, her most secret dream come true, Nick
Granger didn't want her?

"Amy."

Amy's hand jerked. A splatter of the sky-blue paint
her mother had finally settled on for the walls spat-
tered across her shoes and onto the drop cloth beneath
them.

"Sorry, Mom," she said, wiping her brush against
the side of the bucket. "I guess I was sort of day-
dreaming."

Rebecca Johnson cocked her head to one side as
she regarded her daughter steadily.

"Not altogether pleasant dreams, from the look of
it."

Amy looked into her mother's face. The expression
on it was worried but determined. Amy made a split-
second decision. If she was ever going to start con-
fiding in her mother, now was as good a time as any.

"I'm thinking about Nick," she answered. "I feel
like I'm getting sort of mixed messages. We go out
together, have a great time, but . . ."

She paused, wondering how she could tell her
mother what was bothering her without sounding like
she wanted Nick's hands all over her.

That wasn't it at all. It was that she feared the fact
he didn't want to touch her meant he was avoiding
the strong connection that already existed between
them. Something she wanted to cherish, not avoid.

"It's like he's afraid to get too close," Amy finished.

Her mother dipped her brush into the paint and
slowly began to spread it across the shelf Amy was
supposed to have been painting. After a moment,
Amy followed her mother's example. The sound of
the brushes moving back and forth was the only sound
in the room.

"I know I don't have to tell you this," her mother said finally, "because the same could be said of you, but Nick's been through a lot lately, Amy. Coming to live in a new place with a father he hardly knows."

"Spending three days in a box underwater," Amy added.

Then she could have kicked herself. That was exactly the kind of sarcastic response her mother'd always hated.

"Mmm," her mother said, continuing to spread paint. "Or maybe that should be 'Spending three days in a box underwater with some girl he doesn't know inside his head.' "

Amy's mouth dropped open. Her paintbrush slipped from her fingers. It landed on the drop cloth with a wet splat. Her mother turned to look at her, her expression startled. At the look on Amy's face, she laughed.

"I'm sorry, sweetheart. I didn't mean to startle you," she said. "It's just that something I've never understood, and never liked, finally makes sense.

"The way you and your dad talk sometimes. It's not a defense mechanism. It's a coping mechanism. A way to talk about things that really can't be talked about, can't be explained. You know, like black humor in hospitals. It's a way to handle extreme situations."

Amy shut her mouth. "You're absolutely right, Mom," she said.

This time it was her mother's jaw that dropped. "You think I'm right about something?" she said.

Amy's smile quirked up. "I really hope there aren't too many flies in here."

Her mother laughed again.

"There are probably a lot of things Nick can't explain at the moment," she continued, her expression thoughtful once again. "Maybe that's why you can't tell if he's coming closer or backing away. My guess is what he needs is a little more time, that's all. He'll stand still when he's ready.''

''You know something?'' Amy said.

Her mother rolled her eyes. ''On a good day.''

''I really love you, Mom.''

Amy heard her mother catch her breath. And knew that moving across what had once seemed an impossible emptiness of space hadn't been so difficult after all. All it had taken was one first step.

''I love you, too, Amy,'' her mother said. ''And I'll promise you something. I'm never going to let you forget it. I'm never backing up again.''

''Cut it out. You're going to make me cry,'' Amy said.

''As your father would say, tough noogies.''

''Actually, I'm the one who says that,'' Amy answered as she threw her arms around her mother's neck. Her elbow caught the shelf with the paint can on it. It began to sway.

''I'd watch that paint can if I were you,'' said a new voice. ''Somebody in this room has a bad track record when it comes to keeping liquids in their proper place.''

Amy and her mother turned as one unit. Though Amy didn't need to look to know who it was.

''Carl!'' she said. He stepped through the open doorway. Amy and her mother advanced to greet him. Amy bent to retrieve her paintbrush along the way.

''How'd you really like to be a gallant man in blue?'' she asked, waving the paintbrush in the air.

''Pass,'' Carl said. But his gray eyes grinned at her.

''Hello, Carl,'' Rebecca Johnson said, extending her hand to shake his. ''It's a pleasure to see you. What brings you up this way?''

''Just wrapping up some unfinished business,'' Carl

said. He glanced at Amy's mother. "If you don't mind, that is."

"Of course not," she answered. "Do you need privacy?"

"No, nothing like that," Carl said. "I just wanted you to know Steve Dorsey's been bound over for trial, but they haven't set a court date yet."

Amy expelled a breath she didn't even know she'd been holding in. "Will you want me to testify?"

"I'm not sure yet," Carl said. "Dorsey's condition is pretty unstable. He keeps claiming the leader of the Rising Dawn will avenge him and that we'll all be sorry."

Amy shuddered.

"Could he be right?" her mother asked, resting a hand on Amy's shoulder.

Carl shook his head. "I'd say it's pretty doubtful. But I probably don't have to tell you there are still lots of loose ends about that cult. It's not even clear who the leader was."

"No, you don't have to tell us," said Amy's mother.

"So you'll be careful," Carl said. A statement, not a question, Amy noted.

"Yes," said Rebecca Johnson.

"So," Carl said again, his tone indicating an obvious change of subject. His gray eyes teasing Amy gently. "Hear you've been seeing something of a certain former kidnapping victim."

Amy rolled her eyes. *I should have known,* she thought. Carl was up to something.

"Okay, Carl," she said. "What do you want to tell me?"

Carl grinned. He was enjoying every minute of this, Amy thought. "Nick Granger's got a birthday coming up," he said. "Bet you didn't know that."

Amy could feel her stomach start to tingle. Carl

was absolutely right. She hadn't known Nick's birthday was in the near future. But her brain was already wheeling with ideas.

"You're right," she confessed. "I didn't know."

She waited. Carl leaned against the doorjamb and didn't say a word.

"Well," Amy finally said. "Aren't you going to tell me when it is?"

"What's it worth to you?" Carl asked.

"How about your sanity?" Amy suggested.

"I'd tell her if I were you," said her mother.

"August the thirteenth," Carl answered with a laugh. "It's not a Friday. I already checked."

"You're the best detective in the whole world, Carl," Amy said. "And if you tell my father I said that I'm going to have to hurt you."

"It'll be our secret," Carl said. He stood up straight. "Well, I'd better be getting back to Seattle."

"I'll walk you out," Amy said.

In silence, she and Carl walked to where his car was parked alongside the curb.

"Hey," he said, glancing up at the sky. "Looks like it's going to rain."

"But it was clear just a little while ago," Amy protested.

"Welcome to your first summer in the Pacific Northwest."

He hesitated, as if he wasn't quite sure whether he was coming or going.

That's the first time I've ever seen him do that, Amy thought. "Carl, will you tell me something?" she asked quickly.

"Sure," Carl said. But he sounded just a little hesitant, as if he wasn't sure what would happen next.

"Did you drive all the way up here just to tell me about Nick's birthday?"

Carl's face relaxed. "Not really. It was just a side

benefit. The real reason I came was—'' He extended his hand. Surprised, Amy put hers into it, felt Carl's strong fingers close around her own.

"It's been a pleasure working with you, Miss Amy Johnson," he said.

Amy felt a burst of emotion. They'd come a long way since that first day, she thought. All the way from uncertainty, even suspicion, to trust.

She returned the pressure of Carl's fingers. "It's been a pleasure working with you, Detective Carlson. Don't be a stranger, okay?"

She watched Carl's gray eyes light with pleasure. "Okay," he answered. He released her hand, walked to the driver's side of his car, climbed in, and started the engine.

Amy watched as he pulled out into traffic and drove off down the street. He'd definitely decided to trust her, she thought. It was a good feeling.

She walked slowly back into the gallery, wondering how long it would take her to convince Nick to do the same.

twenty-three

What was he going to do about Amy?

Nick Granger sat in his bedroom, in the chair by the window, staring out at the sudden burst of summer rain.

He'd never get used to it, he thought. The way the sky would be clear one moment, the next filled with dark clouds releasing fat drops of rain. It was too sudden, too unpredictable, when all he really wanted was order. Something he could depend on no matter what.

The way he could depend on Amy.

He shot from the chair to prowl the room as he realized what he'd just been thinking. How was he sure he could depend on Amy, aside from the obvious answer that she'd just saved him?

That was just the problem, Nick realized morosely. One half of him was afraid to trust, the other half already did.

He flopped down on the bed, staring up at the ceiling.

What am I going to do about you? What am I going to do about us, Amy?

He didn't want to hurt her, that much was certain. Though he was beginning to suspect he'd done that already.

There'd been something about the look on her face

129

when he'd returned to their seats with two bags of popcorn, not one, that day they'd gone to the movies. As if she'd known he hadn't done it to be polite but because he'd been afraid of what would happen if they shared.

Just being near her was hard enough. There were times when he could almost feel himself literally moving closer to her, the way ferrous metal homed to a magnet.

Part of him yearned for the contact. Believed it was perfectly natural, exactly what he'd wanted ever since that day in San Francisco. Another part of him screamed at him to slow down, put on the brakes.

There'd been so much in his life he hadn't been able to control. Alone, in his box, he'd been totally powerless. It wasn't an experience he was interested in repeating.

Except you weren't alone, his mind countered. *You had Amy.*

She'd been there, inside his head. Offering him hope and comfort in ways he still didn't understand. How could he get close to Amy until he understood and could exercise some control over what would happen next between them?

And so he stayed apart, his mind circling closer and closer around one central question while his body struggled to maintain its distance.

What would happen if their fingers met? If their lips met? If he touched her again? If he told her he remembered her and held Amy Johnson in his arms, would his dream of a soul mate come true, or would he be lost because he'd lost control again?

"Nicholas."

It was his father's voice. There was no other like it in the world. Nick sat up to find his father standing in the bedroom doorway.

"Yes, Father," he answered.

So formal, he thought. *So cold.* Even after all that had happened, Nick still didn't know how to get through to his father. What his father really wanted from him. He wasn't sure he'd ever know.

They both were trying to get closer to one another. He thought he could feel that. But they hadn't gotten very far. The walls that separated him from his father were too firmly in place, perhaps because they'd been there for so long.

"You have a phone call," Elmore Granger said. In one hand he held a portable phone. The hold light was blinking off and on. "I think it's Amy Johnson."

Nick's surprise showed before he could stop it. "You answered the telephone?"

One thing he'd learned was that his father never had direct contact with the outside world if he could help it. As if he thought it would contaminate him, or was beneath him somehow.

Privately, Nick thought it was a weakness, not a strength. One of the things that had made Steve Dorsey's actions possible. He'd never voiced that opinion to his father, though. He didn't see much point.

Elmore Granger lifted one shoulder. "I happened to pass the housekeeper in the hall. When she told me her errand, I offered to deliver the message myself. Nicholas, I . . ."

Awkwardly, his father trailed off. "It would please me very much if you were . . . on good terms . . . with Amy Johnson. We owe her a great deal, you know."

Nick bounded up from the bed, the blood roaring in his ears. "Of course I know it," he answered hotly. "Nobody knows it better than I do, Father. But I'd prefer to spend time with her because I want to, not because you feel we owe her something. I'm not the prize in a box of Cracker Jack."

Elmore Granger raised his hands as if in surrender, and Nick could have kicked himself.

Prize in a box? Way to go, Nick.

"Of course, I understand that," said his father. "I just meant I enjoy seeing the two of you together, that's all. I'm not suggesting you form a permanent attachment."

Permanent attachment, Nick thought as his father's words stopped his hot anger cold. Permanent attachment. Like an add-on to an office building or a parking lot.

Was that the way his father thought about friendship? he wondered. Was that the way he thought about love?

As if his father saw something in Nick's face, his hands moved out toward him, then dropped to hang uselessly at his sides. Nick felt his gut clench as he made a sudden connection.

He never touches me, he thought. After the kidnapping, his father hadn't comforted him, hadn't held him close. Amy was the one who'd done that. The only one.

And how am I responding? Nick thought. *By pushing her away. By building walls between us, just like my father does. If I'm not careful, I'm going to end up just like him.*

Unable to touch anyone, even those he wanted to touch the most.

"I'll take the call," he said, holding out his hand for the portable phone. "Thank you for making me aware of it, Father."

"Nicholas," said his father. "I—"

But Nick was already depressing the hold button and speaking into the phone.

"Amy?" he said, walking to the window, turning his back on the door. "Sorry that took so long."

"That's okay, Nick," her voice said. But she sounded nervous, he thought. Without warning, an image of her rose in front of him as if he'd conjured her up, real as life.

Her short brown hair swinging against her chin. The dimple in her right cheek when she smiled. And her incredible blue eyes that could look right through him.

He closed his own eyes. *See me, Amy,* he thought. *Help me see myself.*

And so he never noticed that his father lingered in the doorway, watching him complete the call. He only heard Amy's voice, inviting him to a dinner in honor of his birthday. His birthday, which his father hadn't mentioned at all.

"Of course I'll come," he said.

"It's not even a Friday the thirteenth this year," Amy answered, the lilt suddenly back in her voice.

And Nick opened his eyes to dazzling sunshine. Just like that, the world outside had changed once more. Raindrops sparkled in the trees, bright as diamonds.

"Yes," he said. "I know."

twenty-four

"Amy," her father said. *"You've already checked that* turkey about a million times."

Amy shut the oven door with a bang. "I just want everything to be perfect," she protested. Though she was so nervous, she didn't think she could eat a thing. "It's Nick's birthday."

"I know it's Nick's birthday," her father said. "You've told me every day for at least a week." Amy stuck her tongue out at him.

"Children," her mother said, breezing into the kitchen. "Stop that. It's rude to quarrel without the guest of honor."

She opened the oven door.

"Not you, too!" cried Amy's father.

Her mother reached in and wiggled the drumstick with expert fingers. "It's done," she said. "Stan, help me get this out of the oven so it can cool down before you carve it."

"How come I have to do all the hard stuff?"

Amy grinned, pleased that her mother was on her side for a change. *I could get used to this,* she thought.

"Because you're the dad," she answered. "I'm going to make sure the table's all right, Mom," she went on, heading toward the dining room.

"She's already checked that about a million times,

too," she heard her father say under his breath.

It was followed by her mother's gentle laughter. "She's excited. Let her alone, Stan."

Amy stood in the dining room, staring at the table. It really did look perfect, she thought.

Fragant candles glowed softly in the center of the table, making Amy's mother's best china gleam as it nestled against her grandmother's best tablecloth.

Amy's parents could hardly believe Amy'd set her heart on a full roast turkey dinner as Nick's birthday celebration. Cranberry sauce, mashed potatoes, the works. Like Christmas in July. She'd hardly been able to believe it herself.

But from the first moment she'd suggested they throw Nick a birthday dinner, Amy had known just what she wanted. Known that what she wanted was just right.

A burst of laughter from the kitchen pulled her back to the present. "For crying out loud," she heard her mother say, the laughter still in her voice. "Don't drop it, Stan."

"I thought birds were supposed to be able to fly."

"Turkey," Amy's mother said.

They're having fun, she realized. In spite of Amy's attack of nerves, all of them were more relaxed than they'd been in days. In months, actually. In all the months since they'd come here from California.

This is my home now. I belong here, Amy thought. The transition was finally complete. The past was just the past.

As if on cue, her parents appeared in the kitchen doorway. Her father had his arm around her mother's waist.

"Looks great, honey," her father said. Amy went to stand beside them. Her father put his other arm around her shoulder.

"Thanks for polishing the silver, Dad," Amy said. "I know how much you hate it."

"You get to do it for my birthday party," her father threatened.

"I thought pizza was finger food," her mother said.

Her father dug a finger into her mother's ribs. "Very funny."

"Well, I guess now I know what Nick and I will do for entertainment tonight," Amy commented. "We'll just watch the two of you."

Her parents smiled at one another. Amy watched her mother's eyes move to rest on her, then on to the shining table and back to her face again.

"Amy," she said softly.

"I know, Mom," Amy said. "Don't get my hopes up too high. You don't have to tell me."

All day long, she'd been giving herself the same advice. Telling herself not to turn this evening with Nick into something too important. But all day, she'd been unable to take her own advice. Unable to shake her deep belief that tonight would be a turning point in their relationship.

"Doesn't it drive you crazy when she does that?" her mother asked.

"You have no idea," her father answered.

"Cut it out, you guys," Amy said.

The doorbell rang, interrupting her. Amy jumped about a foot, her head whacking against the kitchen door frame.

Her father gave a bark of laughter. "Well, I'm pleased to see one of us is cool, calm, and collected."

Amy rubbed her head as she moved off toward the front door. "Thanks for the support, Dad. Remind me to hurt you later."

But her father's reaction had been just right. When she opened the door to Nick Granger, Amy was laughing.

God, but she was beautiful, he thought as he stared at her from the front porch. So alive. Her blue eyes sparkling and smiling. There were candles burning in the house behind her. He could see their soft glow.

Why had he never realized before that she was beautiful?

Because you're a chickenshit, Nicholas Granger. If you recognize how beautiful she is, you're going to have to admit how much you want her.

That was the truth, he thought. In spite of all the push-me, pull-you he'd been doing with her lately, things felt better when he was with Amy. They felt right.

"Hey, Nick," Amy said, her voice just a little husky. "Thanks for coming. Happy birthday."

"Thanks," he said, wishing he could find his balance. "I brought you something," he said, producing the tiny bunch of flowers he'd selected.

Small and white, the blossoms danced along their slender stems like fairy bells. He'd thought they were perfect when he'd seem them in the florist's shop. But all of a sudden they just looked pitiful.

What had he been thinking? he wondered. He should have brought something bigger, more showy. Like roses. Girls liked roses, didn't they?

Amy's face went completely blank. Then she reached for the flowers with fingers that trembled ever so slightly.

"Lily of the valley," she said, her voice filled with something Nick didn't quite recognize. "You brought me lily of the valley."

"It was all they had," Nick blurted out, panic burning in his chest. It dissipated as Amy exploded into sudden laughter.

"Get real, Nick Granger. These guys only bloom for about two seconds in the spring. They must have cost the earth at this time of year."

She flushed then, as if realizing that, for him, money hardly would have been a problem. But she recovered quickly, looking him full in the face.

"Thank you, Nick," she said softly. "Since I was a little girl, they've always been my favorites." She lowered her head to the tiny bouquet and inhaled deeply, her pleasure obvious. "Did you smell them?"

Nick felt his pulse kick into high gear. He hadn't blown it. She loved them.

"You're kidding, right?" he said. "All I did the whole way over here was to smell them."

Their fragrance had filled the whole car. Filled his head, just like Amy, herself, did.

"They smell great," he finally admitted, smiling back at her. "Though I still don't know why I picked them. Everything else just looked wrong, and then the florist showed me these."

Amy lifted her head swiftly. Before she could say anything, her father's voice called out.

"Aren't you going to invite Nick to come in, Amy? I think that's what Martha Stewart recommends for guests these days."

Amy shook her head, her lips pursed with silent laughter. "Won't you please come in, Mr. Granger," she said, stepping aside to make room for him.

"Thank you, Miss Johnson," Nick said. "It would be my pleasure." He took two steps into the living room and stopped cold as Amy closed the door behind him. She almost ran into him as she turned back.

"You can keep going, Nick, you know," she said dryly. "You won't get lost. My house is a lot smaller than yours is."

Nick pivoted slowly to stare at her. "Do I smell turkey?"

Alarm crept into Amy's beautiful blue eyes. "Please don't tell me that you hate it or are allergic."

"No," Nick said. "No, it's—" He paused, his eyes

going to the tiny white flowers she held in her hands, then back to her eyes, deep as the ocean. "My only happy memory of my family together is of one Thanksgiving dinner," he said, revealing more to her than he ever had to anyone.

"Ever since then, it's weird, but—" He gave up, admitted the truth. "Turkey is my absolute favorite. How did you know that?"

"I didn't," Amy admitted. "I just got this idea in my head and couldn't shake it. It just felt right, like the flowers did to you."

Okay, he told himself, *calm down.* There was a perfectly reasonable explanation. But the one that made the most sense was the one he'd spent the most time avoiding.

It wasn't just coincidence. It was because there was something special about what happened between him and Amy.

Almost without thinking, he reached for her. Heard her quick intake of breath as his hand found her shoulder.

Touching her wasn't even like touching another person, he thought. It was like touching some previously undiscovered part of himself, all his own feelings heightened.

He bent his head. Brought his lips to hers. And knew that everything he'd ever dreamed of was possible.

Her lips were smooth beneath his own. He could tell, instinctively, that he'd surprised her. Then he felt the flush of heat as her lips warmed with his own.

Don't ever leave me.

Was it her thought or his own? He didn't know. Didn't care anymore. All he knew was that he wasn't alone or lonely. Not cut off from the rest of the world anymore. At long last, he had a place where he belonged.

"Ahem," said a crisp voice behind them. Nick pulled back to the joy and rueful laughter lighting Amy's eyes.

"Dinner is served," her father said. "Assuming you're done with dessert."

Amy's mortified groan was covered by the quick sound of Nick's surprised laughter.

twenty-five
♌

"*Why don't we have our coffee and dessert in the living room?*" Amy's mother suggested.

Amy pulled her attention back to the present with a jerk. All through dinner, she'd had trouble concentrating, even eating. All she'd wanted to do was stare at Nick.

She could still hardly believe he'd kissed her. Hardly believe she'd been right about what the evening meant. It *was* a turning point between them. And Nick had turned toward her.

I've got to pull myself together before I make a complete fool of myself, she thought. *One kiss and I'm a brainless idiot.*

"Sure, Mom, great idea," she said, standing and picking up her plate. "You menfolk go on ahead, now. Mom and I will put our frilly aprons on and bring out the cake."

"What?" Amy's father said. "No pumpkin pie?" Nick laughed again.

That was at least twice now she'd heard him laugh this evening, Amy thought as she carried plates into the kitchen. Each time the sound got easier. As if he was getting used to it.

She lit the candles on the cake while her mother assembled a stack of dessert plates.

"Ready?" her mom asked.

Amy nodded. "Ready."

Her mom walked ahead of her, dimming the lights. But Amy could see the way Nick's eyes shone, bright as the candles, as her whole family sang "Happy Birthday" to him.

He couldn't remember the last time anyone had sung to him on his birthday. Unless it had been one of the birthdays he'd spent with Pat. Usually, he'd spent his birthday at one of the string of interchangeable summer resorts he'd gone to with his mother. Among total strangers.

He'd loved his mother, known she loved him. But he'd never been able to shake the sense that he wasn't quite at the center of her attention. That she'd spent her whole life looking back over her shoulder, running from something.

He'd never been sure what. Only that her preoccupation had helped make him what he was.

Apart. Alone. Lonely. Unable to explain the thing he, himself, was searching for but didn't really hope to find.

But now he never needed to be that way again. He'd found what he was looking for. He'd found Amy.

Take it slow, a part of him warned as he watched her slicing pieces of the birthday cake he was willing to bet all his father's money that she'd made for him.

Slow down. You're going way too fast.

But if this was a roller coaster, it felt pretty good. He decided he'd sit back and enjoy the ride. He reached to take the slice of cake from her.

"I suppose it would be redundant to mention that chocolate cake is also my favorite?"

Her blue eyes smiled. She hadn't looked at him

much during dinner. But Nick had the feeling he understood why. He'd wanted to stare across the table at her the whole night. Drink in the sight of her.

Whoa, boy, he told himself. *Yesterday, you were afraid to touch her at all. Today, you're acting like some hormone-ridden teenager. Today, you can't get enough of her.*

He slid his feet back against the couch so he could anchor the plate of cake more securely in his lap. Something sharp pricked the back of his left heel. He made a face.

"What?" Amy asked, her attention pulled to him as she served cake to her father.

"I'm not sure," he answered. "I think something just bit me."

"What?"

"I knew it," said Amy's father. "It's the killer dust bunnies."

Nick set the cake plate on the floor, reached beside the couch with his fingers. He pulled out a large notebook.

"Here," he said. "This is it. I must have caught my heel on the end of the metal binding."

"But that's my sketchbook," Amy said, her expression blank. "What's that doing out here?"

"Uh oh," her father said. "I think I must be the guilty party. I was showing the sketches of the garden we'd been planning to your mother. I guess I just set it by the side of the couch when I was through and we missed it cleaning up."

"You sketch?" Nick said, flipping the book open.

"Nick, don't," Amy said.

He heard the thread of urgency in her voice. Ignored it. She just didn't want to be teased, he thought.

"Secrets, huh?" he said, flipping through pages of a layout for the garden. They were good, he thought. Very good. He turned past them. Stopped. Then began to turn the rest of the pages over, rapidly, his heart-beats roaring in his ears.

"Nick," Amy said in a low voice.

The rest of the sketches in the book were of him. Every single one of them.

Some weren't full faces. Just individual features. An eye practiced over and over until she'd gotten it just right. The way his mouth pulled down a little at the corners.

He felt as if he'd stepped into a freezing river, the cold rising slowly upward. All his fears of losing control rising with it.

Why had she drawn him over and over in such loving detail? What did she want from him?

He lifted his eyes to Amy's.

Amy's blue eyes looked wide and startled, her pupils dilated. As if he'd just caught her committing a terrible crime.

He knew he ought to just laugh it off. Knew her parents were still with them, though the whole room had gone deadly quiet. But he couldn't. Something about the way she'd drawn him was too important.

"Why?" he asked.

He watched the muscles in her throat contract as she swallowed convulsively.

"So I could remember. You know, after that day in San Francisco."

He felt his chest contract. That chance encounter had meant as much to her as it had to him. He held the proof right there in his hands.

All of a sudden it was too much. It was way too much.

"What day in San Francisco?"

twenty-six

He didn't want her.

Amy lay in bed, the covers pulled up to her chin. In spite of the heat of the night, she was shivering. The evening, which had started so well, held so much promise, had ended in total disaster.

He didn't want her.

As long as she lived, Amy knew she'd remember the look of frozen panic on Nick's face when he'd seen the contents of her sketchbook. Her brain had screamed at her to laugh it off, offer any excuse.

But when he'd framed his one simple, direct question, she'd been unable to do anything other than honestly answer it. And watch her hopes for the future splinter into a thousand jagged pieces.

He hadn't exactly sprinted for the door. He'd been too well brought up for that. But he'd been unable to hide his dismay, just as she'd been unable to hide her hurt.

And he hadn't been able to hide something else. The thing that hurt most of all.

He'd been lying. He remembered San Francisco as well as she did. But he didn't feel about it the way she did. He didn't want her.

Amy reached for Funny One and rolled over to stare out the window.

All these months, she'd clung to the idea that she and the guy she now knew was Nick Granger were soul mates. That they were meant for one another. In the few times they'd met since Nick's rescue, the earlier meeting in California had never come up. There'd been no time for it to.

Amy had assumed it was because they were focusing on the future, trying to get to know each other. Now she knew the truth. It hadn't come up because Nick didn't want it to.

A soft tap at the door interrupted her troubled reverie. Amy wondered if it would be her mother or her father. The three of them had hardly spoken as they'd cleaned up after Nick's hasty departure. But Amy had felt her parents' concern hovering in the air around her.

"Come in," she called.

The door opened slowly. Her father's head eased around it. So her parents were playing it safe, Amy thought. Sending in the old guard. She was surprised a moment later as her mother's head joined her father's.

"What is this, some kind of kinky dual parenting technique?"

"Do you like it?" asked her mother. "We've been practicing in the mornings before you get up, peering around the bathroom door."

Amy tried not to laugh, because if she did that she knew she'd start to cry. But it didn't do any good. She started crying anyway, the tears welling up and over, and she had no way to stop them.

"Oh, you guys."

She buried her face against Funny One's soft neck. Felt the bed sink down as her parents sat on either side.

"What happened, honey?" her father said. "I don't understand. What was all that about?"

Amy lifted her head, trying not to sniffle. She glared at her father. "How come you always make me cry? I'm turning into a wimp."

Her father smiled ever so faintly. "Nice try. Now answer the question, sport."

Her mother reached into her father's pocket and tweaked the handkerchief out of it. "But first, blow your nose."

"You guys are real bullies, you know that?" Amy said. But she did as her mother instructed.

"I met Nick once before, in San Francisco."

"What?" her dad exclaimed.

"When?" her mother asked.

"The day of the Rising Dawn fire," Amy answered. "I never told you guys. There was a break in the negotiations. I took a walk outside, past the police barricades. I was just standing there, looking over the city, and all of a sudden, there he was. All we did was talk about nothing, but it felt like I'd known him all my life. Like—"

Her voice broke off. How was she going to say this to her parents without sounding like she'd completely lost it?

"Like we were supposed to be together. You know, soul mates."

"Oh, Amy," breathed her mother.

"I know it doesn't make any sense," Amy said. "But, I mean, let's face it, not much about me does. But being with Nick just felt right. As if there were something about him that made him just as alone as I was."

"But you didn't know *who* he was?" asked her father.

Amy shook her head. "It wasn't one of those conversations where you get all formal and introduce yourselves. We just talked. Then I had to go back and—"

She broke off again, knowing she didn't need to go on. They all knew what had happened next. The whole world had exploded.

"Why didn't you tell us about Nick before?"

"I just couldn't," Amy said. "You guys were already so worried about me, I didn't want to make it worse by saying I'd fallen for some guy I didn't even know. By the time I found the picture of him in his room and knew who he was, I couldn't tell you."

"Because you knew I'd pull you off the case if I thought you were emotionally involved," her father finished.

Amy nodded.

Her father rubbed his hand across his face. "You're right," he finally said. "That's what I would have done." He looked across the bed, making eye contact with his wife.

"Your mom and I have disagreed on lots of things to do with you using your talent, Amy. But one thing we've always agreed on: Your safety comes first."

"There's something else we've always agreed on," her mother added softly. "We love you very much."

"I love you guys, too," Amy whispered.

Something lost, something gained, she realized. She was closer to her parents in this moment than she'd ever been. But she'd lost Nick Granger.

"I'm sorry about leaving your sketchbook out, Amy," her father said. "I certainly didn't know what else was in it, or that Nick would react the way he did."

"I know that, Dad," Amy said. "I'm not blaming you or anything."

Her father reached out to ruffle her hair a little. "You going to be all right?"

"I think so," Amy said. "Though it may take a while." She looked from one parent to the other. "He was special, you guys. I made him important to me

148

before I ever went into his mind. I'm not going to get over this in a hurry, so don't expect me to."

Her mother made a wry face. "Thanks for the warning. You want a bedtime piece of cake?"

Amy shook her head. "No thanks."

"We'll see you in the morning," her father said, getting up. Amy watched her parents move toward the doorway. *Together,* she thought. *The thing that Nick and I will never be.* "Try to have sweet dreams, sport."

"I will, Dad," Amy answered.

She listened to her bedroom door click shut. To the house growing still and silent all around her.

I wanted to know what it was like to be like other girls, she thought. *To be normal. Well, I suppose now I do.*

Now she knew what it felt like to have her heart broken.

twenty-seven

𝒮

𝓗e'd hurt her. He hadn't meant to, but he'd done it just the same. Hadn't been able to stop himself. Hadn't been able to hold back the panic. When he'd seen her drawings, only one thing had mattered.

He was losing control again.

Nick drove back to Seattle like a madman. Palms sweaty on the steering wheel, clenching it so tightly his knuckles turned white. Amy's pale face and stricken eyes, flashing before him each time the lights of a passing car struck the windshield.

He'd hurt her. What was he going to do?

Nick knew he didn't altogether have a rational explanation for the feelings that had swept over him as he'd looked at Amy's drawings. But he figured that should come as no surprise.

So much about what he felt for her, *how* he'd come to feel for her, didn't seem rational. Couldn't be explained at all.

All he knew was that staring at Amy's sketches of him had made him feel like he was standing in the middle of yet another sudden Seattle storm. And then he'd heard her voice explaining that the reason she'd drawn them was because of the fact that they'd met before.

He'd lost it then. So totally and completely he still

wasn't sure exactly where he was. She hadn't drawn him just because of what had happened between them in the last month. But because of a meeting that had occurred a whole year ago. One he remembered all too well but didn't understand at all.

He'd been so shaken he'd done the first thing he could think of. He'd lied to save himself. Nick knew he'd never forget what had happened next. The way Amy had gone still, like she'd been turned to stone. And the light had faded from her luminous eyes.

He slowed the car as the final turn to his father's house came up, the engine idling as he signaled to the ever-present security guard. The lock clicked, the gate swung back, crunching against the hedge.

These were the things that had saved him, he thought. The things that only he had known but only Amy had recognized. Without her, he wouldn't be having such confused and painful feelings. He wouldn't be feeling anything at all.

Nick pulled the car into the garage. Crunched across the nutshell path to the house. As he walked through the front door, his father stepped into the entry hall.

"You're home early, Nicholas," Elmore Granger commented in his melodic voice. "Didn't you have a good time?"

"I had a great time, Dad," Nick said, forcing his voice to be casual, easy.

He wondered why his father never called him Nick. The only other people who'd ever called him Nicholas were the headmasters at the various schools he'd attended over the years, and then only when he'd been in trouble.

"Amy's mom's gallery opens soon," he continued by way of explanation. He moved toward the stairs and began to climb them. "They're still doing a lot of work getting it ready, so they have to be up early tomorrow morning.''

"I see," said his father.

"I'm kind of tired, Dad. Think I'll turn in, maybe read for a while," Nick said. He reached the top of the staircase.

"Very well," said his father quietly.

As he hurried along the upstairs hall, Nick caught a glimpse of his father standing in the entry. Elmore Granger stood perfectly still in a pool of light with darkness all around him.

He's completely alone, Nick thought as his footsteps momentarily faltered. Then he picked up his pace, reaching his room in two quick strides, opening the door and shutting the image of his father behind it.

Nick leaned against the door, his heart stuttering. Part of the reason he'd gone to Amy's was because he'd been absolutely terrified he'd end up just like his father.

Maybe it's already too late, he thought. Maybe he was already so much like Elmore Granger that the only thing that seemed more terrifying than being alone was being loved.

On stiff legs, Nick forced himself across the room. He yanked open his bottom dresser drawer and pulled out the sweater Pat's mom had made for him. In spite of the summer heat, he yanked it over his head. Knew at once he'd made a mistake.

Amy had been the last person to wear this, he thought. Wearing this was how she'd found him. He sank into the chair by the window, leaning his head against the cool pane of glass, as an image of his mother rose, unbidden, before him.

He'd always thought his mother had looked back because she was afraid, was running away from something. But now he wondered if he'd been mistaken.

What if his mother hadn't been looking back in fear for all those years. But for the love she'd left behind her.

twenty-eight
𝒟

𝒥*n the days that followed, Amy did her best not to mope.*
And found the effort drained her. But for her parents'
sake, she tried to keep her spirits up. Tried to keep
her feelings from showing.

Her mother's gallery opening was a great success.
Amy was delighted at her mother's pleasure. Her father went back to work, claiming he was so happy it
was just routine that he didn't even mind the boring
paperwork. The days slipped closer to September.

Amy rattled around the house, too restless to settle.
She put her sketchbook not in her bottom dresser
drawer but in the back of her closet, where retrieving
it required extra effort. She didn't want to slip into
the habit of staring at her drawings of Nick. It would
be better, if not easier, to put the whole episode behind her.

She bought a new sketchbook, new charcoal. And
began a series of sketches of her parents, for their
anniversary in November.

And if she still thought of Nick at least a hundred
times a day, she told herself it was a good sign. A
sign that she was like any other girl who'd just lost
the guy she thought she loved. A sign that she really
was normal.

She even told herself she was starting to get over

him. Until the day the doorbell rang and Amy opened the front door to find Elmore Granger standing on her doorstep.

He looked exactly the same, she thought. Standing completely still and composed. She'd never seen anyone with so much self-control. At that moment, she envied him for it.

"Mr. G-Granger," she stuttered.

A faint smile flitted across Elmore Granger's features. "I'm sure this is a surprise, my dear. But I wanted to have a word with you in person. May I come in?"

"Of course," Amy said, feeling like an idiot. She knew Nick's father didn't like to leave his compound, and she'd kept him waiting on the porch like a door-to-door salesman.

"I'm sorry, I didn't mean to be rude," she fumbled. "Please, won't you come in?"

"I'm sure you could never be rude, Amy," Elmore Granger said as she held the door for him.

Amy led him into the living room, gestured toward a chair, and he took it. She settled onto the couch.

"It's a pleasure to see you," she said impulsively.

Nick's father's face lit up. "Why, thank you, Amy. I wish I could be sure you felt the same way about my son."

Amy felt her smile tighten.

"I'm sorry," said Elmore Granger. "Please believe me, I didn't come here to upset you, Amy. I only wanted—"

He paused, and Amy felt his dark eyes watching her closely. The same way he'd watched her when they'd first met. When Nick was in trouble and he'd come to her to save him.

"I wanted to try to explain something about Nicholas," his father continued.

"Please, Mr. Granger," Amy said. "You don't have to do this."

"Now, I thought we settled that," he said in his beautiful voice. "You were going to call me Elmore."

Amy moved her hands in a futile gesture. "Elmore. You don't have to . . . explain about Nick."

"Oh, but I think I do," said Elmore Granger. "You see, Amy, Nick's mother and I loved one another very much. But we could never seem to make things work between us. Finally, we agreed to part. I can't speak for her, of course, but for myself, I always wanted a second chance."

Elmore Granger leaned forward, his compelling eyes on her face.

"That's what I want you to do for Nick. I don't want him to spend his whole life alone, the way I did."

Amy felt as if she were suffocating, drowning in her own fears, her own desires. But it took more than one person to make a reconciliation, a relationship. She knew that all too well.

"Does Nick know you're doing this?"

Elmore Granger shook his head. "No, he doesn't. But I can't say I feel bad about going behind his back. I've been apart from Nicholas for most of his life. I haven't had much opportunity to do what I thought was in his best interest.

"I'm trying to do that now, Amy. I'm asking for the thing Nick can't ask for. For the thing I couldn't ask his mother for: a second chance. Please, just come and talk to him. That's all I ask."

Oh, is that all? Amy thought. He might as well ask her to cut out her heart and carry it to Nick on a silver platter. Elmore was asking her to take an enormous risk.

The risk of putting her feelings on the line once

more, even though there was a good chance Nick wouldn't return them.

And if he rejects me again, she thought, *will I really be any worse off than I am now?*

She didn't think so. Not knowing was the worst. The place where she was now. Even knowing for sure Nick didn't want her would be better than this. The thinking about him all the time. The hope in her heart that refused to die. That told her he still might call.

If he rejected her, she'd be alone. But she'd be free. And if he didn't . . .

"All right, Elmore," Amy said, feeling something in her heart lift and open once more. *I'll give Nick a second chance,* she thought. *I'll give us both one.*

"I'll come with you."

Moments later, Amy sat in Nick's father's Jaguar, savoring the feel of the expensive car as it sped along the freeway toward Seattle. It was a far cry from the cars her parents drove, where half the time something didn't work.

I feel like Cinderella, Amy thought as she listened to the classical music filling the air around her. She thought it was even a waltz.

On her way to the ball, with Elmore Granger as my unlikely fairy godmother. The thought made her smile.

"I'm glad to see you're enjoying yourself," said Nick's father.

"I am," Amy said, and was surprised to find she meant it, in spite of the butterflies fluttering in her stomach.

"Not much longer now," Elmore Granger said reassuringly.

He's so nice, Amy thought. And wondered how Nick got along with his father. How he'd react to what the two of them had done.

Elmore Granger had been so eager to reunite Amy

with Nick that he hadn't even wanted her to take the time to write a note to tell her parents where she was going. They'd be back long before her parents were, he'd promised. Then she could surprise them with her good news.

Amy had felt his optimism catch her up and carry her along. Now they were halfway to Seattle. Halfway to Nick. Amy felt her spirits rise another notch. She was going to make this work, she thought.

Somehow, she'd find the way to convince him they both deserved a second chance. That they belonged together.

The CD came to an end; the lush music stopped. "I'll find something else," Amy said, spontaneously reaching for the eject button. Nick's father reached at exactly the same moment. Their fingers brushed.

And Amy saw the fire.

A solid wall, rising right in front of her. She opened her mouth to scream, but no sound came out. The flames swept closer. Amy's hands crept to her throat.

Then Elmore Granger jerked his hand away. The vision vanished. Amy put her arms on the dashboard and dropped her head down onto them. The silence in the car was so thick she could have carved it like a sculptor does a piece of stone.

Finally, she raised her head. Got her voice to function.

"You're the one," she said. "We thought it was Steve Dorsey, but the whole time it was you, wasn't it? You gave the order that killed those people in San Francisco. Kidnapped your own son."

She could feel the horror of it rising up to choke her. What kind of man was this in the car beside her?

"Would you have let him die, like you did those others?"

"It wouldn't have been necessary," said Nick's father, the man who was the leader of the Rising Dawn.

"His kidnapping produced the desired effect."

He's talking about me, Amy thought, her skin crawling. *About finding out if I still had my talent. About bringing me out into the open. Carl was right. I was the target.*

But they'd all been wrong about who was responsible.

Unable to help herself, she asked the same question Nick had of her. *"Why?"*

"Because you prevented me from doing what I wanted," Elmore Granger answered. "In my whole life, only two people have ever done that. You and Nicholas's mother."

"But I thought—" Amy said, then caught herself. What an idiot she'd been. He'd fed her a sob story of lost love, and like a fish, she'd swallowed it.

"I know what you thought, my dear," said Nick's father. He put a new CD into the player, pushed it in. The sounds of Dvorak's New World Symphony crashed through the car.

New world, Amy thought. *And the Rising Dawn would have been a new world order.*

"You thought exactly what I wanted. I knew a romantic story would appeal to you. That you'd like to hear I had loved Nicholas's mother.

"I hated her," Elmore Granger's smooth voice said. The ice in it made Amy clench her teeth to keep them from chattering. "That bitch took my son away from me. It took me years to find her. I wanted to go after her at first. Bring Nicholas back. But in the end, I decided on revenge."

I don't want to know. I don't want to know, Amy thought. And bit down on her tongue to keep from asking.

"Oh, come," Elmore Granger said as if he'd read her thoughts exactly. "You should never be afraid of information, Amy. After all, knowledge is power."

159

Amy watched as they passed the first Seattle exit. *I've got to keep him talking,* she thought. *Sooner or later, he'll have to slow down. Get off the freeway.*

"What did you do to them?"

"To *her*," Elmore Granger corrected. He smiled as if the memory gave him infinite pleasure. "I sent her money. Enough for her to live well, enough to make sure my son would never want for anything. And so she'd know she'd never be free. Wherever she went, I'd find her."

So simple, Amy thought. As simple as lifelong torture.

"And me?" she asked him.

Elmore Granger flashed her an approving look. "Do you know, in a way, I'm proud of you, Amy. Even now, you have more courage than anyone else I've ever known. Certainly more than that idiot Steve Dorsey. I think knowing you would be good for Nicholas. But it's a risk I can't afford to take any longer. You won't interfere with me again, my dear. I'm going to make very sure of that."

One more question, Amy thought. One more piece to put in place. She folded her arms across her chest, wrapped one hand around the door handle as Nick's father hit his turn signal.

"What about Nick?" she asked. "What happens to him?"

Elmore Granger almost glowed with exultation. "Nicholas has a glorious destiny in front of him," he answered. "One I will soon reveal to him. You needn't be afraid for him, my dear. From now on, I intend to take very good care of him."

He eased up on the accelerator.

Now! Amy thought. She yanked on the door handle and threw herself against the door with all the strength she had.

Nothing happened.

With a strangled cry of desperation, her shoulder tingling in pain and shock, she tried again.

"Stop it," Elmore Granger said sharply. Amy slumped against the door of her Cinderella carriage. Her glorious prison.

"Don't insult my intelligence by such antics," Nick's father continued. "I control every aspect of this car, just as I control every aspect of this situation. Nothing is going to interfere with my plans for Nicholas. Especially not you."

Unbelievably, Elmore Granger's voice became quiet, soothing. As if he were telling her a story to lull her to sleep.

I knew he would be good at bedtime stories, Amy thought. *I just didn't know they would give me nightmares.*

"We are going to a very safe place, my dear," said Elmore Granger's soft voice. "And you will never leave it."

twenty-nine
𝒟

Nick jerked upright, heart pounding, ears ringing.
"Amy!"

He could hear her sobbing inside his head. Slowly, he shook his own head back and forth as the world came into focus around him.

I'm in my own room, he thought. He felt the nap of the corduroy beneath him. He'd flopped onto the bed to read a book, he remembered. He must have fallen asleep reading.

He almost never did that, particularly so early in the day, but he supposed there was a first time for everything.

That was all it was, he told himself. He'd fallen asleep. And dreamed of Amy.

He swung his legs over the side of the bed. Crossed the hall to the bathroom to splash some water on his face.

But it hadn't been a happy dream, he thought. A dream of reconciliation. Instead, it had been filled with terror. Perhaps it was just his own guilt, he thought. Rising from his subconscious to torment him.

If you have a dream like that during the day do you still call it a nightmare? he wondered. He shoved the bathroom door aside with his shoulder.

The images hit him like a two-ton truck. He threw

up his hands, stumbling backward. And watched as Amy slammed herself against a car door once. Twice. Before she abandoned the attempt and slumped over.

He could feel desperation grip him by the throat. Knew it for her desperation. Her bone-deep fear. And then, as if from a very great distance, he heard a voice. A voice he knew.

No! his mind screamed.

The image shut off. Nick found himself standing in the center of his own bathroom, his hands still dripping.

He could hear himself panting like an animal. How could it be possible, the thing he'd seen? The thing he'd heard, the horror of it skirting the edges of his mind like a hunter stalking prey.

It wasn't true. Couldn't be true. Because if it were, then that would mean—

He dried his hands on automatic pilot. Went back to his room, put on his shoes. He snagged his car keys from the top of his dresser, thrusting them into his back pocket. Then he went downstairs and picked up the phone in the entryway.

The same one his dad had brought him the day Amy had called to invite him to the birthday party in his honor. The day his dad had said they owed her something.

His fingers clumsy, Nick punched in Amy's number.

Be home, Amy, he thought. *Please, be home. Make this not be true.*

He listened as the answering machine picked up. Hit the off button with his thumb and cradled the phone.

You're being ridiculous, he told himself. *She could be anywhere. Out somewhere having fun. Helping out at her mother's new gallery.*

Then why could he still hear her sobbing? Feel his

own throat burn with the urge to scream?

Something was wrong. He knew it. Something that had to do with Amy.

Abruptly, Nick came to a decision. It was time to stop fighting. Stop lying and admit the truth. He and Amy were different. They were connected. And they always would be.

Crossing the entry with quick strides, Nick jerked open the front door. He couldn't do what he was thinking of inside that house, his father's house that he feared now would never be a home. He didn't know where his father was. Couldn't risk that he might overhear him, particularly if he was wrong.

Nick backed his car out of the garage, gunned it down the drive. Only when he reached the front gate did he slow down.

But he could feel his heart accelerate even as the car slowed to a crawl. Usually, the guard opened the gate when he saw Nick coming. Today, the gate stayed closed.

"Hey, Nick," the security guard said as he strolled up to the window. Nick's eyes flicked over the name embroidered on the front of guard's uniform.

"Hey," he answered back, striving to keep his tone easy. "Is there a problem, Tom?"

"Well," Tom said, his cheekbones ruddy, as if he were embarrassed. "Your father went out earlier and left pretty clear instructions."

So his father was gone. The fear in Nick's gut became a solid ball of fire. His father had gone out. Amy was missing. He wasn't wrong.

"What did he say?" Nick joked. "That I was grounded?"

Tom relaxed a little. Nick forced himself to breathe, nice and slow. "He did say he didn't want you to leave the compound," Tom admitted. "I'm sorry, Nick."

Nick smiled, amazed his face didn't crack and fall right off. "That's okay, Tom. But it does leave me with a problem."

He paused. Counted to ten inside his mind. Long enough for Tom to start shifting from one foot to the other.

"You know my birthday was just last week," Nick went on.

"Sure," Tom said. "The big eighteen, I heard. Congratulations."

"Thanks." Nick waited again, counting to fifteen this time.

"So, um, what's the problem?"

"My dad's birthday is today," Nick lied. "I think that's the reason he wants to keep me housebound. You know, so I can't do anything last-minute to surprise him. The problem is . . ." He let his voice trail off.

"Oh, I get it," Tom said. "You already set something up."

"Right," Nick said, hoping his relief didn't show. "I just want to go into town and pick his gift up, Tom. I'll be back in half an hour. Did my dad say how long he'd be gone?"

The guard shook his head. "But he did say he'd be a while. I guess it would be all right if you went out. But if your dad asks, you've had that birthday present for a long time."

"Centuries," Nick said. Tom smiled and started back toward the guardhouse. A moment later, the gate clicked open, swung back.

Nick bit the inside of his cheek. *Go slow and easy,* he told himself as he drove through the gate. *Don't blow it now.* If only he didn't meet his father on the road, he'd be home free.

It took fifteen minutes to reach the nearest shopping center. Another five to find the phone booth that he wanted. One away from the street, where his car couldn't be spotted.

He sidled up to the phone booth, dropped his quarter into the slot. Heart pounding as he stared at the front of the phone, he punched in the emergency numbers for the Seattle police department. Listened to the ringing of the phone.

From a throat so dry he never knew how he got the words out, Nick said, "This is an emergency. I need to speak to Detective Carlson."

thirty
D

*I*t was dark.

A dark so dense she could see absolutely nothing. Not even the hand she waved in front of her face. Dark as a grave. A coffin. Dark as Elmore Granger's savage, twisted heart.

He was right, Amy thought. She wasn't ever going to leave this place. He'd hidden her inside her own tomb.

When the first light flared, she thought she was hallucinating. A single match, bright as a bonfire. She'd stumbled toward it, only to see it wink out. A second later, it was replaced by another.

Amy was never sure how many times she changed direction, staggering toward the tiny flames, until she suddenly stood still, realizing the truth.

"I control every aspect of this car," Elmore Granger had said. "Just as I control every aspect of this situation."

Just as he controlled her. And what he wanted was for Amy to know fear. More fear than she'd dreamed was possible.

Because she didn't have to imagine what was coming next. She already knew.

Her knees had given way then, and she'd fallen. Not noticing when the cold floor skinned her hands and knees. One thought streaking across her mind like a comet.

Nick! Where are you?

But she knew it didn't make a difference. He didn't answer. Couldn't answer. Because he didn't want her. Didn't want to accept the thing that was between them. He'd turned away.

She was her only hope, just as she'd been his. But now her hope was all used up. She didn't even jump when the next light flared, mere inches from her right hand.

What was the point? She knew in her soul what was going to happen. Like the members of the Rising Dawn before her, like Brian Newcomb, she was going to perish in flames.

thirty-one
∅

"*Okay, Nick,*" *Detective Carlson said. "Slowly, now.* Go through it again."

They'd started in Detective Carlson's office, but with the arrival of Amy's parents they'd moved to what Nick could only think of as an interrogation room.

While they'd waited for the Johnsons to arrive, Detective Carlson had filled him in on the Rising Dawn, the events that had happened a year before in San Francisco.

And he'd shared his and Amy's father's earlier suspicions. That his own kidnapping hadn't been about getting his father to pay money for him. It had been a way to get to Amy. A way for the Rising Dawn to take revenge.

Just thinking about the ramifications of what the detective had told him made Nick's brain stagger. The place between his shoulder blades itched with tension. It was all he could do not to turn around to face the two-way mirror.

There's nobody there, he thought. *Nobody's watching. Get yourself under control and do what you came here for, Nick. Amy needs you.*

Amy's parents looked like shell shock victims. Pale faces. Enormous eyes. Her mother'd brought an old stuffed clown with her. She sat still, holding it tight. As if that action alone might bring Amy back to her.

"Nick," Detective Carlson prompted.

"I was home, in my room," Nick said in a low voice. "I think I'd tried to read a book and had fallen asleep. When I woke up, I thought I heard Amy's voice. I mean, not her voice, exactly," he fumbled. "Not like she was in the room with me."

He watched as the three adults in the room exchanged glances.

"It's okay, Nick," Amy's mother said. "We understand what you mean."

"I thought I'd had a nightmare at first. Amy was frightened. Sobbing. But when I woke up, she went away. I went into the bathroom to splash some water on my face. I pushed the door open with my shoulder. When I did that, I *saw* Amy. With my eyes wide open, wide awake, I saw her."

He could feel his gut twist as he thought of what he'd have to reveal next. It had been hard enough to tell Detective Carlson. How was he supposed to say the thing he thought he knew to Amy's mother and father?

"She was doing the same thing I was," he continued. "Pushing against a door with her shoulder. Only it was a car door and Amy was frantic. Like she was desperate to get out. Then she sort of slumped over. I heard a voice, like it was right there with her, and I think—"

He covered his eyes with his hand, no longer able to bear looking into the faces of Amy's parents. "I think it was my father."

He was sure he could have heard a pin drop in the silence that followed.

"You think?" said Detective Carlson.

Nick lifted his head then, opened his eyes. There was no way around it. For some reason he didn't understand, he could get into Amy's head the same way she could get inside his. There was a bond between them.

And because of that, he knew the truth.

"It was my father."

Amy's mother made a sound of dismay. Nick saw Amy's dad and the detective make eye contact. Amy's father spoke first.

"The Rising Dawn," he said.

Detective Carlson nodded. "And Steve Dorsey. He said he'd be avenged, that Amy would be sorry."

Nick's throat felt dry as dust. "You're saying I was kidnapped, put into that box, by my own father."

"Actually, you said it," said Detective Carlson. "If your father's taken Amy, there can only be one reason."

"Revenge."

The detective nodded. "Do you have any idea of where he's taken Amy? Has there been any contact since that first episode? Have you tried to reach her in any way?"

"I don't know how to!" Nick exploded. "You guys are the experts on this stuff, not me. Until Amy . . ." He faltered, recovered. "Until a few weeks ago, I didn't even think this sort of thing was possible."

"But now you know it is," Stan Johnson said quietly.

Nick could feel his whole world, every ounce of control he'd tried so hard to hold on to, sliding away from him.

"You can find her, can't you?" he asked Detective Carlson.

"We can try," Carl answered. "But think about what we've got to go on, Nick. Nothing. No ransom note. Nothing to prove Amy's actually been taken. All we really have is you."

"Nick," Amy's father said. "I want to tell you something. Until the night you came to dinner, Amy's mother and I didn't know the two of you had met before. Amy never told us. First, for her own private reasons. Then because she was afraid I'd pull her off the case if I knew."

"Pull her off," Nick echoed. "Why?"

"Because it's not safe to work a case when you're emotionally involved," Detective Carlson answered. "It clouds the investigator's judgment. I didn't know you'd met before. If I had, I'd have pulled her, too."

"That's the standard line," Amy's dad continued. "And usually, it's true. But in the case of you and Amy, I'm not so sure. I think her feelings made your connection stronger. I think it's a big part of why she was able to find you."

Nick could feel something deep inside him breaking into tiny pieces. "I'm afraid," he whispered. "Afraid of what I—we can do."

Her father nodded. "Amy was afraid, too. She'd been afraid for a whole year, ever since the Rising Dawn fire. She thought she'd failed then. That she'd fail you. But she came to realize that she'd been wrong. And the moment she realized she had to let her fear go was the moment she most believed that she could find you."

I don't have a choice, Nick thought. And realized that he'd known it all along. She hadn't given up on him. He couldn't give up on her.

"Okay," he said. "What do you want me to do?"

thirty-two

*S*he was cold.

The hard concrete floor sapped the strength from her body. The hope from her heart. The sharpness from her mind. Amy could feel deep shivers starting in the pit of her stomach, in spite of the fact that she was sitting doubled over, pressing against it with both arms.

At least the lights had stopped. Though what had followed might be even worse. Amy felt as if she were sitting in the center of a time bomb.

Anything could happen at a moment's notice. She had no way to prevent it. No way to know. All she could do was wait, wondering if she had the strength to pray for the miracle to happen.

This is what the others felt, she realized.

All those other victims who had come before her. The ones she'd saved, the ones she'd never known. All of them must have known a moment just like this one.

The moment they knew they were never going home.

Elmore Granger had gotten her to follow him willingly. Subdued her to get her past his own security guard. Amy didn't know exactly where she was, but she was sure she was on the Granger estate. The one place on earth he felt most in control.

How long will he keep me here? she wondered. Toying with her while he took his revenge. The revenge of the Rising Dawn.

Dawn. A thing Amy knew she'd never see again. She tried to conjure up an image of it in her mind. But in its place rose something else. Nick's face. The way the light of laughter filled his eyes.

Nick, Amy thought. *Where are you now?*

If she'd taken it more slowly, hadn't frightened him away, would there have been a way to prevent this thing that was happening to her?

Stop it, Amy! she told herself. If she was going to die here, never seeing her family again, never seeing Nick, she was going to let go of blame the way she'd released her fear.

Alone, in this dark place, she would admit that, even if it didn't make sense, she loved Nick. Would always love him.

She closed her eyes against the terrible darkness. "Nick," she whispered. "Nick."

She almost didn't realize when the miracle happened. The one she'd been afraid to pray for. She felt the other presence move into her mind.

Amy?

Amy opened her eyes.

He's doing it, she thought. *Elmore Granger. He's found some new way to torment me. Make me lose my mind. Kill me with my greatest hope.*

Amy, it's Nick, the voice said, stronger now. *I can feel you, so you must be there. Can you hear me? Say something.*

Amy's lips parted. *Nick.* Her mouth moved again, though it didn't make a sound.

Amy, I've got Funny One, Nick said. *Your parents brought him.*

174

Amy felt her coldness leave her in a great rush of warmth. This wasn't a trick, a way to break her mind. Only her parents knew about Funny One.

Nick! her mind cried.

Amy, thank God. I was beginning to think—

It's all right, Nick, Amy said. *I'm here. I'm fine.*

Amy, Nick said, *I don't think we have much time. I'm not sure how long I can do this mind thing. So I want you to do what we did before. Don't try to tell me. Just run the movie. Show me what happened so we can find out where you are.*

All right, Nick. I'll try. But it—there's something you should know first.

How can I tell him? she thought.

It's okay, Amy, Nick said. *I already know. Don't think about me, how I feel. Let me think about you now. I don't want to lose you, Amy. I want to find you. Do you hear me, Amy? I want you.*

I hear you, Nick, Amy thought.

Eyes wide open, heart burning with hope, she stared into the impenetrable darkness and let the pictures flicker in her mind.

thirty-three

ঌ

"*S*he's somewhere on my father's estate," Nick said. "That's all I know. He must have done something to put her out just before they reached the gates. That's when the images shut down."

He didn't tell the others about the rest of what he'd sensed. How terrified she was. How cold and alone. He kept it to himself, just as he did his own resolve.

He was going to find her. Bring her out safe. And nothing was going to stop him.

But in spite of his resolve, initiating contact with Amy had left Nick almost nauseated from exhaustion. His head pounded like a pile driver. But he fought his pain down the same way he fought his panic.

"I want to go back to the compound," he went on. "Confront my father."

"I'm not sure that's a good idea," said Stan Johnson. "We have no idea what your father's planning, Nick. Besides—" He broke off, rubbing a hand across his face.

"We can't forget he's willing to make big sacrifices," finished Detective Carlson quietly. "Usually involving other people's lives."

"All the more reason for me to confront him," Nick countered. "I want him to know that if he hurts Amy, he hurts me, too. You have to understand some-

176

thing about my father, Detective. He's totally into control. Think about the way we live. The security cameras everywhere, the motion detectors. Shaking him up may be the only way to get to him.''

Carl's head came up like a dog on the scent.

"What?" asked Amy's mother.

"The security cameras," Carl said. "They usually back up to tape or disk.''

The pounding in Nick's head let up abruptly. "And that could show us where Amy's hidden on the grounds.''

"Do you know where the monitors are?" asked Amy's father. "The backup system?"

"In the guard station at the front gate, I think," Nick answered.

"Okay," said Amy's father. "We go with plenty of backup but leave it out of sight, outside the gate. We can discuss the details along the way.''

"I should take my own car," Nick said. "He'll know I've gone by now. The security guard said he didn't want me to leave today.''

"I wonder why," Detective Carlson said.

The sickness roiled in Nick's gut. "Maybe it was supposed to be my initiation day.''

"God," Amy's mother said. "Oh, God, my daughter.''

"We're wasting time," Detective Carlson said. "Let's go get her.''

Hold on, Nick thought. *Hold on, Amy. We're coming.*

Half an hour later, he watched as the security guard at his father's front gate moved toward him.

Tom was gone, Nick noticed. No doubt because his own absence had been discovered. Had Tom been replaced with someone loyal to his father? he wondered.

Willing to sacrifice himself as Steve Dorsey had?

He could only hope it wasn't true. That the guards at the front gate were of the rent-a-cop variety.

Police backup teams were spread out along the road behind him, out of sight of his father's security cameras. Amy's mother waited in one of the cars.

Detective Carlson and Amy's father were wedged like sardines in Nick's trunk. It had seemed the best way to get them through the gate.

He rolled down the window, smiled at the guard. "Hey," he said, keeping his eyes on the man's face. "What happened to Tom?"

The security guard seemed nervous. "Your father— that is, Mr. Granger—fired him. Tom disobeyed his instructions."

"That's right," Nick said easily. "He let me out. I guess my father wanted me to stay at home. Well, I'm back now. I'll talk to him about it."

"I'm supposed to search your car," the security guard blurted. His eyes dropped as if studying Nick's paint job.

Nick's eyes flicked to the man's name tag. *Time to tough it out,* he thought.

"Just open the gate, George."

George's head jerked up. "But your father's orders."

"Screw my father's orders," Nick said. "I'm eighteen years old. I'm a legal adult. I don't have to follow my father's instructions. You either open the gates or I drive through them. You decide." Nick slid the car into reverse, revved the engine. "Do it fast," he said.

George threw up his hands in disgust. "Okay, okay," he said. "Man," he muttered as he walked back toward the guardhouse. "Now I'm gonna lose *my* job."

He hit the button, opening the gates. Nick put the car in first and eased it through. He rounded the first curve, out of sight of the gatehouse cameras, stopped, and popped the trunk.

"If your father's been watching, he'll know something's up," Carl said as he shook the kinks out of his legs. "Let's move."

When Nick rounded the final corner and pulled up in front of the house, his father was waiting on the front steps for him.

Nick switched off the car, got out slowly, trying to ignore the way his heart was roaring. He only hoped he could play this right. Shake his father's iron-clad control.

Not my father, he thought. *Not the way Amy's is to her.* This man was a stranger, a foreigner. He always had been and he always would be.

"Nicholas," Elmore Granger said, "what is the meaning of this behavior?"

"That's funny, Dad," Nick said, leaning against the car insolently. "I was just about to ask you the same question."

His father took a quick step forward, then pulled himself up short.

Gotcha, Nick thought, resolving to push harder.

"You will not speak to me in that tone of voice," Elmore Granger went on. "And you will not countermand my orders."

"Cut the crap, Dad," Nick said, pushing himself upright. "I know who you are. I know *what* you are. And I know that you've got Amy Johnson. What did you do, Dad? Put her in a box underwater? Let me tell you something. You disgust me."

"Nicholas," said his father, obviously shaken.

That's right, Nick thought. *Get it through your head. You don't control me.*

"You don't understand," his father said.

Nick gave a bark of harsh laughter. "Well, why don't you enlighten me? What were you trying to do,

179

establish a new world order so you could leave it all to me? So I could grow up to be just like you?''

"Yes," Elmore Granger said, his eyes lighting with a strange inner fire. "Yes, that's right, Nicholas.''

Nick moved toward his father slowly. It was all he could do not to reach out and take hold of him. To hurt Elmore Granger as Elmore Granger had hurt so many others.

"I want you to listen to me very carefully, *Father*. I am never going to grow up to be like you. I hate you and everything you've done and stand for. You're not my father. You never were. You never will be. As far as I'm concerned, I'm an orphan. I have no father.''

"No," his father said, his face ashen. "No, Nicholas, you mustn't say such things. You must listen to me.''

"I don't want to hear anything you have to say," Nick answered through clenched teeth. "Except one thing. *Where is Amy Johnson?*''

"Somewhere you will never find her!" Elmore Granger screamed.

He whirled, lunging for the house. Nick launched himself toward him. They went down together on the hard front steps, Nick's father beneath him.

Images exploded in Nick's head. Things more nightmarish than anything he'd ever dreamed. The horror of what his father was, the things he'd done, rose up to overwhelm him. He opened his mouth to scream.

Strong hands pulled him backward. He lay on the steps, panting, gasping. Dimly, he was aware of Detective Carlson looming over him. Amy's father, pinning Elmore Granger against the bricks.

"The lap pool," Nick gasped. "It's the lap pool.''

And swore he heard Detective Carlson say, "You're joking.''

180

thirty-four
D

*S*he'd moved to a corner of the room and put her back against the wall so she could see whatever was coming. She didn't know if Nick would find her in time or not. But she knew one thing.

She would no longer make things easy for his father.

When the first crack of light appeared, she didn't know whether help had finally arrived or whether her life was about to be over. After the darkness of the room, any kind of light was painful.

She cried out, putting her hands over her face. If this was Elmore Granger's revenge, he'd chosen it well. If she was going to die now, she'd do it just like Brian Newcomb.

And then she heard the sound of running feet. Her name being shouted out, over and over.

"Amy. *Amy!*"

Her hands still over her eyes, blind to everything but the wild beating of her heart, she called out.

"I'm here, Nick." And felt his arms around her.

"I still can't believe it," she said a little while later.

She and Nick were still on his father's estate. While the house and grounds were being searched with a fine-tooth comb, they'd walked down to the water. Side by side, but not touching. He hadn't touched her since he'd pulled her from her prison.

Well, Amy thought. *Things are back to what passes as normal.*

"I can't believe it's really over."

"It is if I have anything to say about it," Nick said. "I don't think I could take much more of this."

Amy stared out across Lake Washington. *He rescues you and you bring him here,* she thought. *Great choice, Johnson.*

I wonder what she's thinking? Nick wondered. Did she still want him? Would she even be able to look him in the face, or everytime she did would she only see his father?

Amy had been found in a hidden bunker that had been built alongside the lap pool. A room wired to explode, ending her life in a ball of fire. Elmore Granger had intended her to die as the members of his cult had died.

But it hadn't happened. Because his son had found her.

Amy's reunion with her parents had been tearful, joyous. Even Carl had pulled her into his arms for a quick hug before going off to attend to Nick's father.

At the sight of Amy, living proof that his plans were dead, Elmore Granger had finally lost it. He was sitting in the back of a police car, handcuffed.

What's Nick thinking? Amy wondered. Was it about his father? Though they'd been together since her rescue, Nick hadn't talked much. Amy didn't know if he blamed her for the disintegration of his family.

She didn't know how he felt about the whole situation. About her. The fact that he'd saved her didn't really mean anything. It didn't mean he loved her.

I have to do this, she thought. She had to leave

things clean between them. Had to leave him free to walk away—if that was what he wanted.

"Nick," she said softly, "I want to thank you. And I want to apologize. I know you must have thought I pressured you earlier. I didn't mean to. I just . . . couldn't help the way I feel."

"Don't," Nick said suddenly. "I'm the one who should apologize. I lied to you, Amy. I never forgot that day in San Francisco. I just didn't know how to let it matter to me."

He was going to have to do it, he thought. The hardest thing he'd done in his life, including facing down his own father. He was going to have to ask Amy for a second chance, knowing he had no way to control the outcome.

"Amy," he said, "if I ask you, will you do something for me?"

Amy felt her racing heart stumble in her chest. *Here it comes,* she thought. The moment when he tries to let me down easy.

"Of course," she said, hoping he never knew how hard she was working to keep her voice even. "What?"

He reached for her hand even as he spoke.

"Touch my hand."

Their fingers met, and Amy was surrounded by a world of vivid color. In her whole life, she'd never seen anything as beautiful as this. As the feelings she and Nick Granger had for one another.

He felt dizzy as the colors mingled with the wave of relief washing over him. He hadn't driven her away.

"Okay," he said. "So far so good, huh?"

And heard Amy give a spurt of helpless laughter.

"I was hoping we could do something else," he said.

His eyes have gold flecks in them, she thought.

Ones she'd never noticed before, bright as the end of any rainbow.

"Oh, yeah? What's that?"

"I was hoping we could start over. Give ourselves a chance to discover what this really is." He made a face. "Give me time to learn to cope with it."

Amy felt her heart turn over. A second chance, she thought. The thing his father had dangled like a carrot in front of her. And now Nick was asking for it for himself. For them both.

He jiggled her hand a little. "You haven't said anything," he remarked. "That makes us guy-types kind of nervous."

"But us girl-types love to see you sweat."

Amy saw Nick's lips curve into a smile. Felt her own lips curve in answer. He leaned down, his intention plain on his face. Just before his lips brushed hers, she told him the thing he needed to know.

"You read my mind, Nick Granger."

In the Enchanted Hearts series, romance with just a touch of magic makes for love stories that are a little more perfect than real life.

In Janet Quin-Harkin's Love Potion, the fourth title in the series, T. J. and her dad move to her eccentric great-aunt's house in Beverly Hills. There T. J. discovers a book of spells and some latent powers within herself and immediately puts them to work on the guy she perceives to be her true love—who also happens to be the hottest TV star this side of Rodeo Drive.

Love Potion
𝒟

"*So* do you think you'll be able to come, T. J.?" Morgan asked as we paused at the flight of steps leading up to my front door. In case you think I live in a mansion or something, I'd better say right now that it wasn't just my front door. My father and I had a tiny apartment in an old brownstone in what my father thought was Greenwich Village but actually wasn't. As with most things in our lives, my father just missed out on this goal, too—by a couple of blocks.

I kicked against the bottom step, staring down into the blackness of the basement, and tried to imagine living in a place where you never saw the sun, ever. At least we didn't live down there—not yet. It could happen, though.

"I'd really love to," I said, "but I don't think I can."

"But you have to," Morgan pleaded. "It will be boring out at the beach by myself. And I won't have the courage to talk to lifeguards if you're not there. I wonder if that blond guy from Sweden will be there again."

"Sven, you mean?" My face lit up for a second, then fell.

"It's no use. I have to get a job this summer or I'll have no money."

187

"There are jobs out at Sag Harbor," Morgan said. "Maybe you could work at that great little ice cream shop. Remember where they gave us the double scoops and the sprinkles?"

This was all getting too tempting. I shook my head firmly. "I'd love to come stay with you for a couple of weeks, but there's no way I could leave my dad for the whole summer. You know what he's like. He'd forget to eat. And I really have to get a real job, Morgan. I have to start saving for college now. How can my dad afford it?"

I went on kicking the step. It made a nice, hollow, rhythmic noise.

"Bummer," Morgan said. It had been her favorite expression for the whole five years I'd known her, since we were assigned desks next to each other in sixth grade. Neither of us knew anyone else in the entire school, so we were kind of thrown together. Then we found that we actually liked each other. I enjoyed having her as a best friend—she was smart and funny and always had great put-downs for the doofuses (as she called them). She was almost as big a TV addict as I was, being left alone a lot, like me.

We got along great, even though our lives were totally different. She lived with her mom, who was a famous fashion designer, in a light, airy penthouse apartment with a view across to Hoboken. They spent their summers out in Sag Harbor, in a neat gray salt-box house overlooking the water.

I lived with my dad, who was a writer—the kind of writer who didn't make money from his books. Not that he was a bad writer. He wrote pretty well, but it took him forever to write a book. He'd written three in his life so far. He was forty-two years old. An output of one book every thirteen years is hardly cooking. And it doesn't pay the rent. That's why I shopped exclusively at thrift stores and I was great at finding bargain bags of not-too-squishy vegetables at the market. And it was also why I needed to make good money during the summer and couldn't go to the beach with Morgan.

"You couldn't persuade your dad to write a quick screenplay?" Morgan suggested hopefully. "Or even an episode of *Days of our Lives*?"

I spluttered out laughing. "My dad? *Days of our Lives*? I don't think so somehow. He hasn't a clue about what people do in the twentieth century. He only knows about how people killed each other in the Civil War." That's what he wrote about—boring old battles, long ago. "And anyway," I added, "if he was going to write for any TV show, it would have to be *Surf City*. Then maybe I'd be able to go to the set and meet Brandon Healey."

Morgan shook her head. "This crush on Brandon Healey is becoming obsessive," she said.

"I can't help it. He's my dream guy, Morgan. I'd do anything to meet him."

"Dream on," she said. "He's in L.A. and you can't even afford to go to Long Island." She grabbed my jacket suddenly. She always was overdramatic. "You have to come somehow, T. J. If you don't go, I don't go."

"Don't be dumb. Do you think your mom would let you stay in the apartment alone?"

"Double bummer," she muttered. Then she brightened up again. It took a lot to keep Morgan down for more than a second. "We'll have fun if you can only come for two weeks. This year we'll definitely get to meet Sven. Your dad can survive for two weeks alone, can't he?"

"I guess. It's not like he notices I'm even around when he's working. Of course, I'd have to come home once a week to buy groceries or he'd die of starvation."

Morgan nodded with sympathy. "Only a month until summer vacation. I can't wait, can you?"

I glanced at my watch. "Gotta go," I said. "The *Surf City* rerun starts in five minutes. I think it's the one when Brandon saves that dying dolphin."

"Oh, that was awesome. I'm going to go watch it, too."

"Call me later."

"I will. 'Bye."

I waved as I ran up the steps. Then I dragged my feet up the three flights to our apartment. My head was a jumble of thoughts. I wanted to go with Morgan to Sag Harbor so badly, but I really needed a job in the city. Junior year meant proms and looking good. I didn't want to be the only person who went to her prom in a Salvation Army dress.

I was out of breath as usual by the time I reached our front door. I opened it and went in.

"Yoohoo, I'm home," I called, as I always did.

No answer.

This was strange. My father usually came out of his trance long enough to call back "Hi honey. How was your day?"

I pushed open his study door. He was sitting at his desk in front of the window, holding a sheet of paper in his hand, staring at it.

"Earth calling Father," I said. "Your beloved daughter has arrived home. You're supposed to tell her how glad you are to see her and how much you've missed her."

"What?" He looked up with a dazed expression on his face. His normal expression was already pretty dazed, only this was even more spaced out than usual. Then he focused on me. "Oh, hi, honey. How was your day?"

"Fine, thanks, how was yours? Did you get a lot of research done at the library?"

He shook his head. "I just got the most extraordinary letter," he said, waving the piece of paper at me.

"Bad news?" I asked cautiously. Most letters that came to our place were bills.

"Not at all. Good news, I think. I'm not quite sure what to think at this moment. It's from Aunt Sophia."

"Aunt Sophia? I didn't know I had an Aunt Sophia." I peered over his shoulder to look at the elegant but spidery handwriting.

"My aunt, not yours," he said. "My father's only sister."

I read the address at the top of the page. "Beverly Hills? She lives in Beverly Hills?"

Dad nodded. "She used to be a movie star," he said as if he were saying "She used to be a checker in Safeway."

"A movie star? Are you serious? What was her name?"

"Sophia Baker. She used her own name."

"Never heard of her."

"You wouldn't. It was long, long ago now. She was very famous during the thirties, but then she met a man, married him, and gave up acting, just like that."

"How romantic. She sacrificed all for the man she loved."

"And then he was killed in World War Two," Dad went on. "And she never got over his death. She shut herself away in their mansion and became more and more of a recluse. From what I've gathered she never goes out of her mansion anymore. She never sees anybody. That's why I'm surprised she wants to see me now."

I took the letter from him. "Dear Nephew," it began. "I am getting on in years and it occurs to me that I have led a unique life. The facts of this life should be recorded before I am too old to remember them. I am told that you are a fairly competent writer"—I glanced at him and grinned—"so you would suit my purpose very well. I would prefer that such a task was not entrusted to strangers. You will help me write my autobiography. I'd like you to come as soon as possible as I am anxious to begin."

I looked up. "Boy, she has some nerve, doesn't she? Who does she think she is, the queen of England? She expects that you're going to drop everything for her."

He smiled. "She always was that sort of person. I only saw her when I was a small child, but I remember her bossing everyone around."

"How come you haven't kept up with her?"

"It was she who stopped keeping up with us. She quarreled with the family and hasn't talked to anyone for years. I'm surprised she wants to see me now."

"Blood is thicker than Barbara Walters?" I suggested.

He laughed. "And doesn't cost as much."

"She's going to pay you for this, isn't she?"

We both looked at the letter. "She doesn't say," Dad said at last.

I read out loud: " 'You will be welcome to make your home with me for as long as it takes to write the book. Please notify me of the date of your arrival. I will expect you shortly. Your aunt, Sophia Baker. P.S. I understand there is a child. You may bring her as long as she is well behaved and doesn't touch things.' "

"Doesn't touch things. I like that," I spluttered. "What does she think I am—two years old?"

"I don't imagine Aunt Sophia has had much experience with children," Dad said, smiling at me fondly. "She had none of her own. And she hasn't been outside that big old house for years."

"Does she really live in a mansion?"

"I suppose you could call it that. It was certainly big enough."

"A mansion in Beverly Hills." I sighed. "This will be so cool, Dad. When are we going?"

"I haven't decided whether to accept her offer yet."

There were times when I wanted to shake my father. This was one of them. "Are you crazy? We're living in this crummy apartment where the hot water heater doesn't work and we're living on day-old bread and week-old vegetables and you say you haven't made up your mind whether you want to live in a mansion in Beverly Hills? Let me make it up for you. Start packing!"

"But my book on Gettysburg," Dad said weakly.

"It can wait, Dad. It's not like Gettysburg's going anywhere." I put my hands on his shoulders. "And maybe this book will make you famous. You'll make so much money you can do what you like for the rest of your life. You can even send your talented daughter to a good college."

He nodded seriously. "That would be nice," he said. "But how would you feel about changing schools?"

"Changing schools? I thought it would just be for the summer."

"I'm sure it will be longer than that. The lease on this place isn't up until July, so we couldn't go anywhere before that. Then we'd have to put stuff in storage. . . . I can't see us getting there before August, just in time for you to start a new school year."

"Oh," I said, quickly running this information through my head—a new school for my junior year, no Morgan—pretty scary stuff. But then, it was a school in Beverly Hills, wasn't it? And it wouldn't be forever. . . . "This is such a great chance for you,

Dad. You have to take it. I guess I'll survive slumming it in a mansion."

"Then I'll write back to Aunt Sophia," Dad said.

"And I have to call Morgan and tell her." I sprinted to my room and snatched up the phone.

"What are you calling me now for?" Morgan's angry voice demanded. "Brandon's standing in the ocean, keeping the baby dolphin's head above the water. Why aren't you watching?"

"I've got incredible news," I said. "Listen to this, Morgan. We've been invited to California by my great-aunt, who is an ex–movie star, and we're going to live in a mansion in Beverly Hills."

"Yeah, right," Morgan said. "What was your real news?"

"That's it!" I screamed. "We're going to California and"—suddenly it hit me. California? Hollywood?—"Morgan," I yelled, "I'm going to meet Brandon Healey or die in the attempt!"

Cameron Dokey lives in Seattle, Washington, where she wishes it would stop raining. Staying inside does give her lots of opportunities to do things that she enjoys. Like taking naps with her three cats, reading books with her three cats, and being a couch potato with her three cats while they watch *Felicity*, *Charmed*, and *Buffy the Vampire Slayer* together.

Cameron had a great time writing *Lost and Found*, because it gave her a chance to put two of her favorite story elements, romance and suspense, together. Love's a mystery anyway, right?

In addition to *Lost and Found*, Cameron is the author of twelve other books, including the *Hearts and Dreams* series from Avon Flare.

Love stories just a little more perfect than real life...

Don't miss any in the

enchanted ♥ HEARTS
series:

READ ONE...READ THEM ALL—
The Hot New Series about Falling in Love

MAKING OUT

by KATHERINE APPLEGATE

Gripping, true-life accounts
for today's teens

Edited by
Beatrice Sparks, Ph.D.

IT HAPPENED TO NANCY

She thought she'd found love...
but instead lost her life to AIDS.

77315-5/$4.99 US/$6.99 Can

ALMOST LOST

The True Story
of an Anonymous Teenager's
Life on the Streets

782841-X/$4.99 US/$6.99 Can

ANNIE'S BABY

The Diary of Anonymous,
A Pregnant Teenager

79141-2/$4.99 US/$6.99 Can

GET READY FOR THE STORM...

AVONtempest

PRESENTS CONTEMPORARY FICTION
FOR TEENS